Kākāpō Keeper

For special A to special Z and special
B B E E L & N in between — GB

First published by OneTree House Ltd, New Zealand

Text © Gay Buckingham
978 19900350 50

All rights reserved. No part of this publication may be reproduced, stored in a retrieval system or transmitted in any form or by any means, electronic, mechanical, photocopying, recording or otherwise, without the prior permission of the publisher.

Cover design and illustrations: dahlDESIGN
Printed: Your Books

10 9 8 7 6 5 4 3 2   2 3/2

'We're alive, Andrew,' says Mr Henry.

'Yes.'

'And I think we are probably very lucky to be able to say that,' he adds.

'What do we do?' I ask. I think I am too scared to move.

'Well, I'd like to say that we will go back to the boat and go home, Andrew, but the second noise we just heard was, I think, a landslide.'

Rocks and earth and trees sliding down a mountain would be very noisy.

'If it has slid right down into the fiord it will have caused a tidal wave. If it has caused a tidal wave then I'll be very surprised if we still have a boat to go home in, as the wave will have swamped and swept everything away in front of it. And of course we don't know if we have a home left, either, for that matter.'

I let it sink in.

No boat.

Miles from civilisation.

Kākāpō Keeper

GAY BUCKINGHAM

A novel based on the work of
Richard Henry and his assistants on
Resolution Island: 1894–1900

CHAPTER ONE

Date: Mid-July, 1894

Bird tally: 0

Injuries tally: 4

- *Sprained (well maybe only twisted) left ankle, from jumping out of Pūtangi in such a rush because of Lassie and the weka family.*
- *Sore back, from carrying piles and piles of things we'll need to survive here.*
- *Millions of sandfly bites, they seem to get any part of you they can find.*
- *Worst of all, my brain is hurting, because I can't work out how I am going to get away from this horrible, lonely place – and because I don't know how I could have been so stupid as to agree to come here at all.*

This is what's been happening:

'Lassie! Lassie! You bad dog! Sit! Confound you! Sit dog, sit!'

Mr Henry stops rowing *Pūtangi* towards Pigeon Island, drops the oars and half stands up to roar at our dog. 'Sit Lassie! Sit! Bad dog!'

The boat is laden down with everything from tinned food and bags of flour and sugar, to books, to clothing, to fishing gear. Not far behind us, *Hinemoa's* dinghy has a load of timber, roofing iron and tools. We are landing our supplies, being splashed by rough waves and trying not to get wet – or even worse, get our blankets or food wet – so haven't been watching Lassie. As we get close to shore she suddenly leaps out of the boat, in the blink of an eye is on the beach, and, in a quick flurry of movement, has a bird in her mouth.

'Andrew! Grab her.' He's yelling at me now and I haven't done anything wrong. 'Quick, boy. Quick. Jump out and grab her! Lassie! Sit! Sit!'

I clamber over canvas and sacks and boxes and

plunge out, making the boat rock so violently it could be swamped – or Mr Henry tipped out – and land awkwardly in water nearly to the top of my legs. I limp-rush to shore, getting really wet, but am too late. There is black and white Lassie, with soft brown down round her mouth, looking very pleased with herself and expecting praise from me. On the ground in front of her is the blood, feathers and broken-necked bodies of two grown weka and their young one.

Three birds killed in what seems like less than half a minute.

Mr Henry usually speaks and moves quietly and precisely, but he is still bellowing at Lassie as he beaches the boat, throws the anchor roughly onto the shore, jumps out, and rushes to where I am holding her by the collar.

'Bad dog, Lassie!' he yells again and grabs her roughly from me. 'Andrew, shove the boat up a bit higher and throw a line round that tree to hold it.' He gestures at a huge driftwood tree trunk. 'Then bring some rope over here so we can tie her up.'

I secure the boat to the tree, take a bit of strong cord off one of our boxes and take it over to Mr Henry, who ties Lassie to a small beech tree near the water's edge.

'When we get unpacked, you'll be wearing a muzzle,' he says to her furiously. 'And what's more, from now on we'll make sure she never goes anywhere without one,' he tells me.

We spend the next two or three hours unloading our stores. It's back-breaking work. After we unload *Pūtangi* we have to trudge everything up to a mound well above the beach where we are going to make camp.

When the boat is empty we go back to *Hinemoa* and start filling her up for a second trip, this time taking tents, canvas, and scientific equipment like the rain gauge and compass. Meanwhile seamen from the dinghy of the *Hinemoa* also make a second trip,

Weka (rail)

Has repetitive call that is a loud 'coo-et.'
Usually heard at dusk and in the early evening.
A scavenger - will eat almost anything.

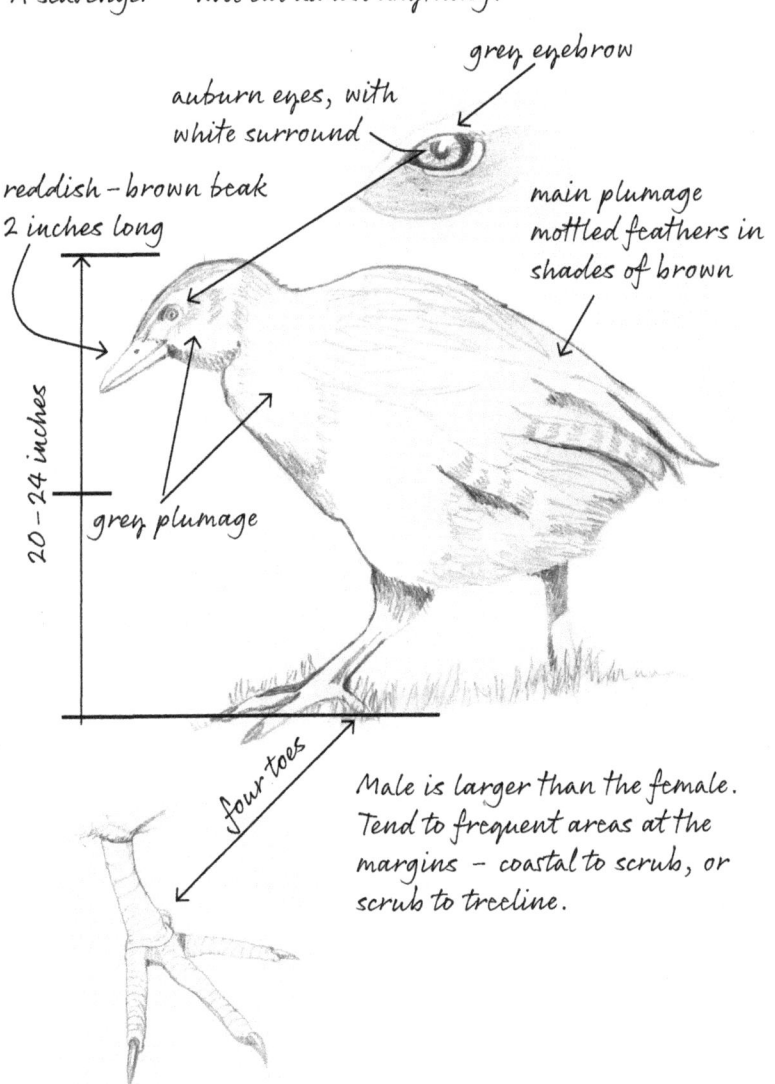

- grey eyebrow
- auburn eyes, with white surround
- reddish-brown beak 2 inches long
- main plumage mottled feathers in shades of brown
- 20-24 inches
- grey plumage
- four toes

Male is larger than the female. Tend to frequent areas at the margins - coastal to scrub, or scrub to treeline.

unloading tools, wire netting and bricks this time. There is a misty rain starting and stopping while we are carting things so we have to wear oilskin jackets and cover our things with canvas, or drape tents over them.

'Hey Lassie, I know you didn't mean any harm,' I say to her – or something similar – each time I take a load past her. Occasionally I just cluck my tongue at her. I really love Lassie and feel sorry for her because she thought she was doing the right thing. After all Mr Henry has trained her to catch birds. Actually, despite the way Mr Henry has been shouting at her, I know he is really proud of her and loves her, too.

'You're a good dog, aren't you Lassie?' I say as I pass.

I can't help loving Lassie, she is the best dog in the world, but killing the weka is the worst thing she could possibly do because we have come to this miserable place in the middle of nowhere to save birds. The thing is, I understand her disappointment because I think I'm feeling as disheartened as she is. I had no idea it would be as remote and lonely as this. Or the weather so dull and damp.

We're going to be living here all alone, miles away from everyone else, because Mr Richard Henry has been appointed Chief Conservator at Dusky Sound. I am his paid assistant (sometimes Mr Henry calls me 'Chief Assistant to the Chief Conservator', crinkling his eyes) and we're supposed to catch kākāpō and kiwi living on the mainland of New Zealand and move them to Resolution Island, which is inside Dusky Sound.

They'll be safe on the island because it is nearly half a mile away from the mainland and separated by wild, swift and very dangerous Acheron Passage, which no predator could swim across. We're doing this because they are disappearing from all parts of the country and may become completely extinct like the dodo, a bird I read about in one of Mr Henry's books on the way here.

It is by a famous man called Darwin. One day people might read a book about saving kākāpō and kiwi, written by a famous Assistant Conservator named Andrew Burt.

Andrew Burt: that's me.

Now everything has been unloaded and we are having our last night on *HMS Hinemoa* after two long, seasick weeks getting here. The *Hinemoa* is a steamship and it's her job to drop off supplies to all lighthouses in the south of New Zealand, so on the way to Dusky Sound we stopped at lonely, remote places like Cape Saunders and Centre Island. You could say we're like the lighthouse keepers, because from now on we'll be relying on the *Hinemoa* to bring our stores and mail, and take away our letters, including Mr Henry's reports. In fact you could call us kākāpō keepers.

I wish I could leave on the *Hinemoa* when she sails in the morning. Coming here was a mistake. It's so far away from everything, and there is absolutely not another single person living here within miles and miles. I must have been really stupid thinking it would be exciting to come catching birds. When Father and Mr Melland agreed I would work as Mr Henry's assistant, all they talked about was camping in the bush and rescuing birds.

No one talked about how it feels to be so far away from home. No one said there wouldn't be another human being within a day's sailing. (Let's not talk about how long it would take to walk to civilisation – except there isn't a track to walk on anyway.) Nobody mentioned the drizzly weather. No one told me about the sandflies here that bite, bite, bite, every single bit of human skin they can find. Just like no one said Mr Henry and I are only going to be camping for a short time – that in fact we are going to build a whole house and make a garden.

I *hate* gardening!

I first heard about the housebuilding and gardening

when I came on board *Hinemoa* before we departed Dunedin.

'We will build a rough camp using canvas, to begin with. We will camp in that while we inspect all of Dusky Sound to be sure of the very best situation for our permanent house,' I heard Mr Henry telling the captain. 'After that we will build a boat shed and establish a garden.'

He's embarrassing when he talks like that, you'd think he was talking to the mayor. I didn't know how to say housebuilding and gardening is not what I was expecting, so I said nothing.

Breakfast is over, we're off the *Hinemoa*, on the *Pūtangi*, and heading to Pigeon Island where we left everything yesterday. Mr Henry is rowing, Lassie is sitting at the front of the boat, I'm slapping at sandflies and watching the *Hinemoa* sail off towards Five Fingers Peninsula. But I don't have time to talk about how long it will be until we see another human being

– which is not until she returns in three months' time. By the time she is disappearing around the end of the peninsula we are nudging the boat onto the shore.

'Right, Andrew, time to start learning the ropes,' says Mr Henry after we pull and push the boat above the tideline. He's trying to make some sort of punning joke because he adds 'this is the painter,' pulling the rope from the front of the boat. He says the knot I used yesterday takes too long to undo and shows me how to tie a special knot, 'a bowline', as we secure it to the same large, driftwood stump.

We head up the slope towards the mound where we left everything. The sandflies are worse than yesterday. To protect my neck I have my collar pulled up and tucked into my hat which I've pulled down over my ears. I have my sleeves pulled right down, my hands in my pockets and my trousers tucked into my socks.

Lassie, despite the muzzle, is dancing with

eagerness as we approach the stacked building materials, the bundles, chests, and cases of clothes under canvas, the bags of food and equipment carefully covered by canvas tarpaulins.

'All right, Lassie, all right. Don't get excited. There won't be any birds sheltering under the tarpaulins,' says Mr Henry. Another attempt at a joke.

But Lassie is getting excited. She starts making little whimpering noises, doing a sort of whistling, snorty panting, and running from one heap to another, but also pawing at the mounds and humps under the covers. She concentrates on pushing her nose where there are food boxes and barrels and makes snuffling noises as she tries to get under the covers.

Mr Henry pulls a large square of canvas off one pile she is particularly interested in.

'What the –' he exclaims.

We stand, motionless, staring at what lies under the cover. I'm not sure what I'm seeing. It's as if the ground is moving – it's dark and writhing – have we left our possessions on a nest of something? The noise hits us at the same time as I realise what it is: rats.

Rats.

Heaps of them. Panicked by the light and the dog. Squirming over each other. Tails waving. Little pink eyes, ears on top, mouths open, feet like hands. They screech, showing tiny, sharp teeth, and skitter away. Lassie, her muzzle firmly in place, lunges amongst them, shoving and slugging them with her head and chest.

The rats scatter and are gone.

Mr Henry and I look at each other. He looks stunned. I am horrified.

They have left droppings all over the ground, on the packing, the boxes, the casks, the bundles. They have been all through our things.

I really can't believe I have to stay here.

This is a disgusting place.

Rats Identification

Kiore –
(rattus exulans, Polynesian, Pacific)

Believed to have come here from Pacific with Maori settlers.

Tail same length as body.

small ears and eyes

white belly fur

Feeds on the ground and in trees.

Small oblong pellet dropping.

Breeding: is food dependant, occurs in spring & early summer, up to 6 litters a year.
Nests: solitary, tree stumps, rocks, burrows.
Swimming & climbing: poor swimmer, good climber.

Ship – (rattus rattus, black, roof, house rat):

Tree climber, nests in trees, hunts at night. Prehensile tail is longer than head and body.

light and slender
large ears

Breeding: most common species, one pair can produce 3000 descendants over 12 months.
Nests: because good climber prefers roofs, trees, walls.
Swimming & climbing: poor swimmer, good climber.

Droppings oblong with blunt ends – about ¾ inch long.

Thick, heavy body covered in grey or dark brown fur

small ears

small eyes

<u>Norway</u> –
(Rattus norvegicus, sewer, common, brown, wharf)

Hunts at night.

tail shorter than body

paler fur

Breeding: breeds all year round, up to five litters a year.
Nests: lower levels, basements, underground holes, sewers, very occasionally in ceilings.
Swimming & climbing: good swimmer, doesn't climb much.

<u>Tracks</u>

front foot
toes widely spaced 4 and circular →

back foot has 5 toes, forward toes 3 almost in a line →

CHAPTER TWO

Date: End of July, 1894

Bird tally: 0

Injuries tally: 3

- *Millions of sandfly bites. Mr Henry says not to scratch them as that is how they get infected, but I think I must do it in my sleep.*
- *Sore back, from trying to sleep on the wooden floor of the tent.*
- *My brain still hurts from trying to work out why I agreed to come – and how to get away.*

This is what's been happening:

We've been here two weeks. The rain's eased and I'm on the beach by *Pūtangi*, wishing I could launch her and leave. I look as if I'm doing fitness exercises. I fling my hands up to my face, smack my wrist with one hand, smack my neck, smack the other wrist with the other hand, reach down to one foot and then the other – to tuck my trousers into the tops of my socks, making sure my ankles are covered – smack the back of my neck, smack one hand ... The sandflies never stop consuming me.

Have I talked about the sandflies? No one would believe how many there are, or how bloodthirsty. I had never thought about what bloodthirsty means – *thirsting for blood* and that's what they do, they thirst for blood and drink it. Thousands – millions – of these tiny insects thirsting for my blood, and thousands – millions – drinking it. And each sandfly leaves an awful, maddening itch where it has bitten into my skin to *suck out blood.*

At least rats eat rubbish. What use are sandflies?

Sometimes I feel like calling this place Misery Sound, not Dusky Sound.

I miss my family. They don't know about the rats, the sandflies, the seeping rain, or that we haven't even started looking for birds. They don't know

Damper

Flour, with half the same amount of water and a pinch of salt mixed to a stiff dough. Squash down flat in the oven. Cook for half an hour over hot ashes. Can add ashes and cinders piled over it. Brush off the ashes when done. Can be wrapped round stick & held in fire but you end up burnt on outside & doughy in middle. Camp oven best as the damper not burnt, doughy, or ashy. Better if baking soda and/or cream of tartar added. Better still if sultanas added. Best of all if with syrup on it.

Queen Pudding Recipe

Break old damper into bits and spread with jam or sprinkle with sultanas and place in the camp oven which has been greased with fat. Beat 3 or 4 penguin eggs, add half a cup of sugar and a small tin of milk, pour over damper. Bake 3 quarters of an hour in camp oven, not too hot.

Bellows used to blast air at a fire to help build the flame.

nozzle

valve

alternative set up

I'm lonely and that Mr *Boring* Henry hardly talks. I wonder what they're doing.

'Bring in the hall chair to make seven seats at the table,' Mother used to say and after grace we would all sit down together and talk a lot and eat a lot – stew with dumplings, roast meat and gravy and pies. There'll be only six people at home now, and if something is to be shared, it'll be easy to divide it into quarters for my four sisters. I hope they miss me, but the girls will be busy doing things, going to school, talking with friends. They like cooking, too. I'm remembering jam tarts, queen pudding, sponge cake.

Plain fish or tinned meat with damper is what we mostly eat here.

That's another thing nobody bothered to warn me about – that the food would be awful – or that I'd be expected to cook damper, which is like a big scone, cooked in the embers of the fire, and we eat that instead of bread. It's not hard to make – but it's not good to eat, either. Nobody said I would be lonely for my family, or that I'd miss my friend Arthur. Yesterday Mr Henry discovered rats had eaten the laces out of his boots. I laughed but Mr Henry didn't.

Arthur would have laughed.

'Right, Andrew lad,' says Mr No-Jokes Henry, who has come down the track to the beach. 'Time for us to get to know our way around this place.' He indicates the mast, which has been lying on the beach ever since we arrived. 'Give me a hand with this.'

I grunt as I lift it. It's hard to balance upright.

'Steady, steady now, lad,' Mr Henry keeps saying. It's tricky manoeuvring it into position on the boat and seating it securely. Mr Henry shows me how to tighten the forestay and shrouds to hold the mast in place, then unrolls the sail and starts lacing it onto the boom.

'We've built a rat-proof storehouse, got the tent set up, and cleared the rocks to make boat launching easier. Now we'll investigate the whole of Dusky

Sound.' He speaks as he works. 'We need to find a place where we can build a house that's sheltered from storms with a good boat harbour and close to Resolution Island, where we'll release the birds we capture.' He looks over at me for a moment. 'Better stow the oars and bailer, Andrew.'

I get them, thinking that though I came expecting to camp, the canvas and wood-floor camp we've put up isn't at all comfortable and perhaps a house wouldn't be so bad. And, at the rate we're going, we'll be here for a long time before we have caught enough birds, so we might as well be a bit drier and cosier.

'We can look for the best landing and camping places at the same time, for when we go bird hunting. Find the billhooks ... and the compass, lad.'

'You mean we're going searching, but not for birds?' Now he is attaching the sail to the rope running up the mast. The billhooks were with the oars. I'll have to go up to the tent to get the compass.

'Our primary task will be to assess the bird population in an attempt to discover which areas are inhabited by the most numerous kākāpō, kiwi and roa.'

If Arthur were here we'd wink at each other when he uses words like *assess* and *numerous*. Mr Henry carries on talking.

'We'd better explore Resolution Island and see what birds are already living there. Telescope as well, Andy. As soon as we can we must make tracks on the island so it is all familiar territory and easy to traverse when we return to check released birds.'

Familiar territory, traverse. More grand-sounding words. More jobs to do instead of bird catching. It's a wonder he's not saying we must build the cottage and a boat shed before we can start birding. Or build a jetty and six paved roads and a couple of castles.

And catch some wild horses!

'So, let's get to know our way around the whole of this place. Pack some damper and a tin of beef, get the oilskins. Call Lassie. Let's go.'

We begin investigating Dusky Sound.

I'm learning to row. Mr Henry teaches me how to brace my body with my legs, and how to watch a particular spot on the shore so I row in a straight line.

I'm learning to sail. He shows me how to pull a rope *'line'* up the mast, to set *'trim'* the sail, and hold the rudder to keep us on course. I now know *'tacking'* means turning the front *'bow'* of the boat so the wind is on the other side of the sail but if the sail swings across – because we have kept the sail at too tight an angle, or the direction of the wind behind us has changed – we have *'gybed'*.

I like having boat skills.

And I'm beginning to think Dusky Sound isn't so bad. It doesn't rain *all* the time, sandflies don't *always* come out, and not *every* bit of the fiord is so badly infected with rats.

We explore all the coves, crevices, gullies and hills

as we look for birds, house sites, landing places, and camping spots with water. So much to check for. So many different places to go to do the checking. While we move about in the bush we hear the songbirds above us and see the little wrens and robins fluttering about, hoping for insects. When we are on the water or shore there are weka and gulls everywhere. We see flocks of parakeets and kākā all the time, but when we do start catching these ground birds – if we ever do – it's going to be very different. We hardly ever see them. There might be a scuttling movement if we surprise them, but none of them – roa, kiwi and kākāpō – make any noise in the daytime and, because their colours match the bush, they are very hard to pick out. Lassie has more success as wearing a muzzle doesn't stop her finding the birds, just stops her hurting them.

We go to Facile Harbour, where the beach is covered with tawny beech leaves, marbled with streaks of red, khaki and copper. Oystercatchers fossick at the high-tide line, reminding me of the blackbirds at home, which pull at straw on the garden in the same way.

We go to Luncheon Cove.

'Captain Cook named it because he had lunch here and really liked the spot. You will, too,' says Mr *Knowledgeable* Henry.

I do like Luncheon Cove. It's completely surrounded by bush and there are no sandflies! You could hide here and no one would ever see you. I can imagine Arthur and me hiding here and watching for smugglers – or even spying on sealers. Sealing's against the law now but we could work to protect the one or two which might still exist, just like we are trying to protect the kākāpō and kiwi.

I'm learning far more than how to catch birds.

While we are sailing Mr Henry tells me more about kākāpō and kiwi, which can't fly to escape the dogs and rats that have arrived in New Zealand.

'To make matters worse,' Mr *Teacher* Henry says,

'runholders and farmers have released mustelids – stoats and weasels and ferrets – to catch rabbits which are eating grass needed for sheep. 'Mustelids are absolutely deadly killers of ground birds,' he adds.

Sometimes it's very quiet. When there's no wind and the water is completely still, like a lake, there's a feeling of solitude and mystery around us. We know waves may be crashing on the outside headlands and cliffs, but in the fiord a great silence descends. The tranquil water and bush beside us, with the high, high peaks straight above, immense and timeless, give me a peaceful feeling through my entire mind and body. It is so quiet I think the whole world could forget we exist.

Today it is like that – completely calm, too calm to bother with the sail, which is loosely tied along the boom. The sun is shining, fairly weakly, yes, but it is shining, and the light makes everything look open and welcoming. We haven't gone very far: I've rowed for about an hour and we're alongside a little creek emerging from a gully. Mr Henry thinks it looks a likely place.

'Fresh water, nice bit of flat land for the tent,' he says. 'Let's pull in and see if there are many birds in the bush.'

We beach the boat, throw the grapnel over a fallen tree and set off to follow the creek up the gull. Lassie, wearing her muzzle, trots happily ahead of us. The vegetation in this gully isn't as thick as some we've been in, it's mostly beech trees looming over the pockets and mounds of moss. The odd tawny-coloured leaf floats down, there's some long trembling warbles from bellbirds or tui – the two often confuse me – and there are fantails and robins flicking around us, checking our movements, looking for insects we may have disturbed or dislodged.

There are lots of little wrens twitching like knights on a chessboard, going two paces forwards for one sideways, and from dark to light or light to dark. We go quite a long way up the gully but it's a pleasant climb. Suddenly Lassie stops dead still.

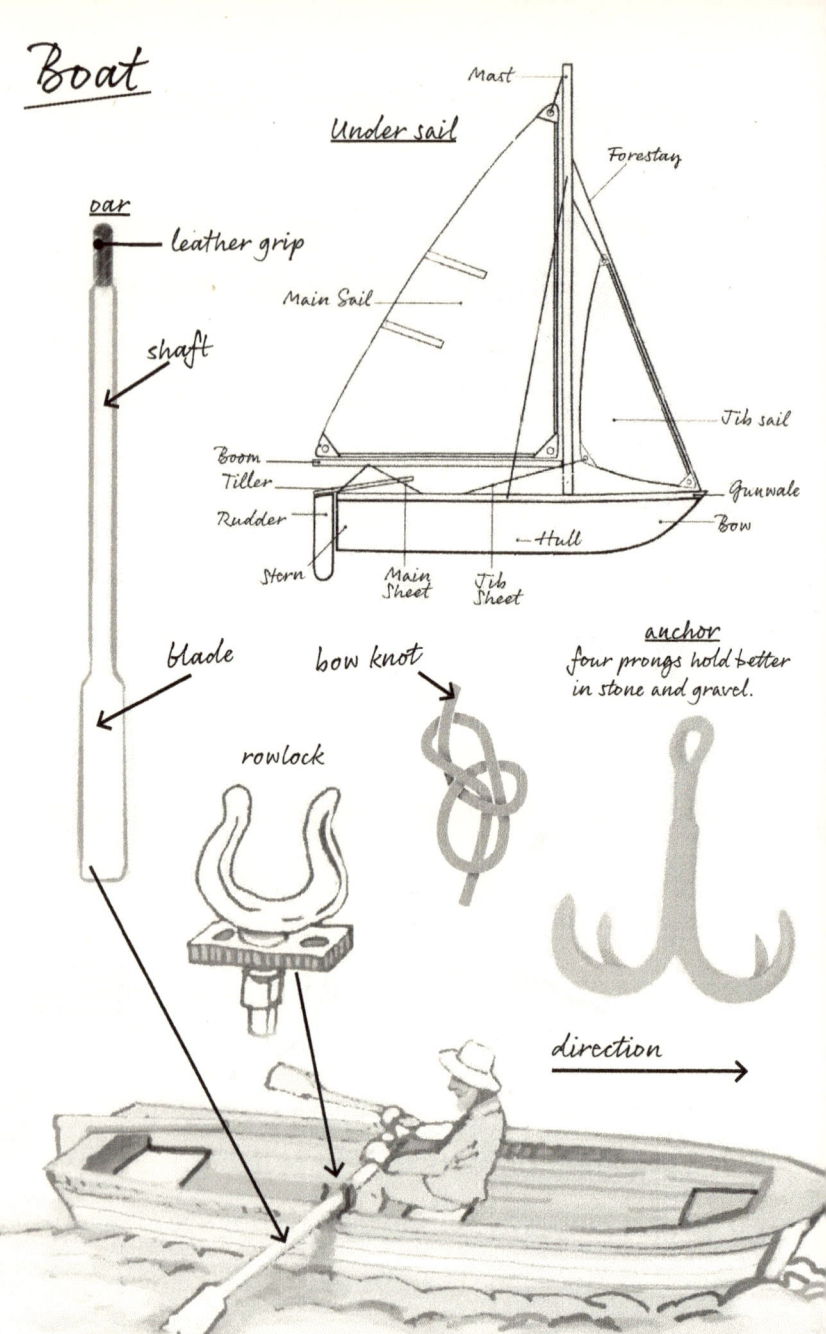

I think she's heard or smelt a bird. Kākāpō? Kiwi? But she's not moving in any direction. I stop, too, waiting to see what she will find. Mr Henry almost walks into my back. In the same moment I become aware of a piercing silence. It sounds silly, to say a piercing silence, but this quietness is far louder than the everyday bush noise of close and distant bird calls, trees hushing and sighing, creaking branches, frilly water ripples. The silence lasts for perhaps five seconds.

Suddenly I feel the ground moving. I am falling, righting myself, leaning, upright again, falling. But now the trees are doing the same, falling, bending, leaning. Now I realise the ground is causing it, it's heaving about, pitching and rolling, as if there is a giant underneath us, and the giant is starting to wake up and is stretching. Then I hear the giant begin to moan, no, to roar. The giant is roaring, the ground is a sequence of rolling waves, the trees are like water swishing this way and that way and moving, moving, moving, and I can't hear anything except a roar that gets bigger and louder and bigger and louder and I think I am going to die. I am going to die and will never see my parents or sisters and I cannot believe there could be such a loud noise and Mr Henry is grabbing me.

'Get down, boy, crouch down and if a tree falls its branches might protect you,' he is yelling. 'Down, boy, down!'

I've heard him shout at Lassie like that but I am not a dog.

The roaring is lessening and I hear sharper noises, trees cracking and splintering and crashing and snapping. Suddenly. It stops. There is still the odd crash and crack but the moving has stopped and so has the roaring. I look for Mr Henry. For Lassie. They are squatting close by. We are all still here. I look at Mr Henry. His face is white. He moves his mouth and though I can see he thinks he's talking to me, no words come out. I nod at him.

He nods back at me.

'Mr Henry?' I say.

'Earthquake, Andrew.'

I'm not sure I know what an earthquake is. I think I have heard of them.

Mr Henry clears his throat. 'We used to get them when I lived in Marlborough.'

I feel something. I look down. Somehow Lassie has managed to get over to me and is pushing her whole body against me. For reassurance I suppose.

Now there is another roaring. It is different from the last one. I look at Mr Henry.

'Oh, no.' He looks all round. 'Oh, of course. Stay put Andrew, do nothing. Just wait.'

We wait. We wait forever. The new roar gets louder. There is a thundering and echoing, crashes and bangs coming from everywhere.

It sounds as if – it *feels* as if – the whole of Dusky Sound, every single stone and tree and beach and island and hill and mountain of Dusky Sound is being shaken in a world-sized echo chamber.

Then that noise dies down.

Then it stops.

Then Lassie whimpers.

Then Mr Henry asks if I am all right.

Then I notice a bird making an alarm call.

No other birds answer it.

Then I cough a couple of times and say Mr Henry's name. I don't trust myself to try to say more than that.

'We're alive, Andrew,' says Mr Henry.

'Yes.'

'And I think we are probably very lucky to be able to say that,' he adds.

'What do we do?' I ask. I think I am too scared to move.

'Well, I'd like to say that we will go back to the boat and go home, Andrew, but the second noise we just heard was, I think, a landslide.'

Rocks and earth and trees sliding down a mountain would be very noisy.

'If it has slid right down into the fiord it will have caused a tidal wave. If it has caused a tidal wave then I'll be very surprised if we still have a boat to go home in, as the wave will have swamped and swept everything away in front of it. And of course we don't know if we have a home left, either, for that matter.'

I let it sink in.

No boat.

Miles from civilisation.

I look at Mr Henry. I can see he is thinking exactly what I'm thinking.

'We'll head down,' says Mr Henry. 'But be very careful, there'll be branches and trunks loose and falling at random. Keep your eyes and ears open.'

We start to make our way precariously down but find it's not difficult to walk. What is difficult is that every now and then the earth shakes a bit, or grumbles, and I think it's starting again. There are a lot of uprooted trees but they are hooked up and caught on each other. The moss is still in mounds and slumps. A few more birds start to call.

It doesn't take long to get to the bottom of the gully but I notice that Lassie no longer leads, she's following me. And I'm following Mr Henry.

The place where we landed is unrecognisable. Rocks, stones, branches, trees have been thrown up on the place we left the boat. There is no longer anywhere we could erect a tent, in fact the creek seems to be gone, there is just scoured-out bank with saplings and branches and water spilling down. We stare at that then look out over the water. The calm fiord has gone, the whole bay is full of debris from trees and branches. The water is dark with soil and sand and seems to slop unevenly, this way, that way.

Mr Henry speaks.

'How can that be?'

I follow the line of his gaze.

Suspended on a tree near the washed-out creek bed is *Pūtangi*. She is hanging with her bow pointing towards the ground and her hull facing us. She does not appear to have any holes in her. We stand and look, then, without speaking, rush – as quickly as we can, for there are a lot of branches and obstacles to get round – to the boat. Her mast, and the sail that was attached to it, has gone but as far as we can see she has suffered no great damage, and unbelievably, though the grapple is nowhere to be seen, the rope from the bow is still attached and dangling.

We set about retrieving her. It takes a while.

I hold the rope and keep her nose outwards as Mr Henry manoeuvres away the branches she is lodged on, thus allowing her to drop to the scoured-out slope below. We have the strength of Titans as we drag her to the water and launch her. Lassie jumps aboard before the boat is even halfway into the sea.

The tide is going out and we use broken branches as paddles to get back to Pigeon Island. It is the longest trip of my life. When we get there our tent with its wooden floor is the most beautiful thing in the world.

We will have to order a new sail when the *Hinemoa* comes but Mr *Capable* Henry says we will make a new mast ourselves. We brought a spare set of oars with us.

CHAPTER THREE

Date: July–September, 1894

Bird tally: 0

Injuries tally: 4

- *Grazes down one side of my face from where I slipped getting out of the boat and landed on a rock (healing).*
- *Goose-egg bump on my head from before the earthquake, when Pūtangi gybed and the boom swung and caught me. It's gone from dark purplish-black to blue, and is now a greenish-yellow and getting smaller.*
- *Every part of my body is covered in sandfly bites. I reckon they get under my blankets and wait for me to go to bed, then hide in my shirts and wait for me to get dressed.*
- *Blisters on my hand from rowing (they have burst and really hurt).*

This is what's been happening:

'We've survived yesterday's earthquake,' I say to Mr Henry. 'But do they happen in Dunedin? Will my family be all right?'

'I think that because it was so strong where we are, if they felt it at all in Dunedin it would have been just a single, little jolt.'

'So they won't know it's just luck that we aren't dead, or marooned without a boat?'

'Correct, Andrew.'

I stare at him. We could be dead and no one would know.

Yet another thing I wasn't warned about.

'On the other hand, you'll have a lot to tell them when you get back.' He grins at me and almost winks.

He's right. I can't wait to tell Arthur about the dangers of Dusky Sound!

In our conversations Mr Henry never mentions bird catching. I'm desperate to start and could list the things I've learnt in preparation – getting around in

Tawaki
(Fiordland Crested Penguin)

Has a black head, is a blueish-black on its upper body, with white underneath.
Found in coastal forest, scrub and caves.
Feeds on krill, octopus, squid and small fish.

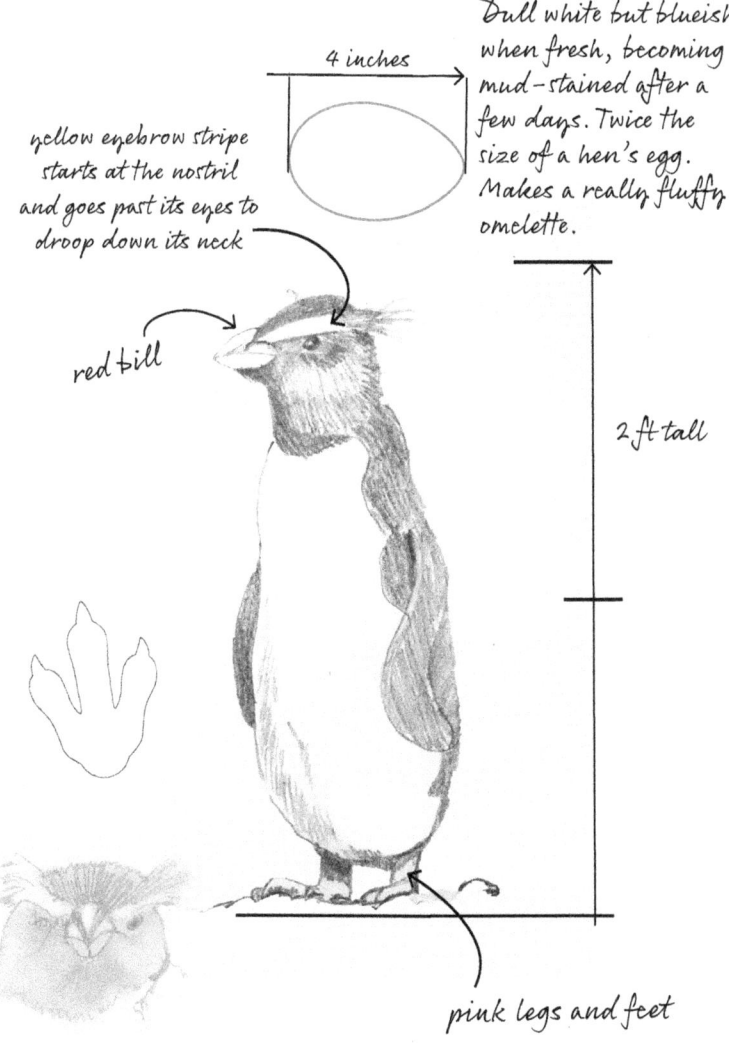

4 inches

Dull white but blueish when fresh, becoming mud-stained after a few days. Twice the size of a hen's egg. Makes a really fluffy omelette.

yellow eyebrow stripe starts at the nostril and goes past its eyes to droop down its neck

red bill

2 ft tall

pink legs and feet

the boat by using both oars and sail, cutting tracks, finding good camping places and most of all, checking where the birds are plentiful. On top of that I'm learning to cook, to build (the storehouse is standing up to the terrible Dusky Sound winds very well) and, not so good, Mr Henry is teaching me to garden. I *hate* gardening.

I also realise how very valuable Lassie is. Pushing through this wet bush, steep gullies, tangled vines, creepers and ferns to catch birds is really difficult for humans but she is so agile, she can get through anything at speed. That is also a problem. We use the billhooks a lot of the time, to slash at trees and push through tangled areas, and she could so easily dash between the billhook and what we're hacking at and get badly cut. We are too far away from anyone or anything to get help for her. I mention this.

'That's true,' Mr Henry agrees. 'But, Andy lad, it's also true that if anything happens to you or me, we are too far away from anyone or anything to get help.'

He's right. Nobody had pointed that out. I add it to the list of things I wasn't warned about.

'That's why Mr Melland wanted me to have an assistant – you, in other words,' he adds. 'In case of a mishap.'

'But what use would I be? I couldn't row to Bluff and get a doctor. You could die.'

'No lad, you couldn't row to Bluff. And yes I could – could die I mean. But you'd be here to tell the captain of the *Hinemoa* what happened and why you only need half rations.' Mr *Jokester* Henry's eyes twinkle and he chucks Lassie under the chin. 'Anyway, we won't let anything happen to you, eh Lassie, best dog in the world.'

Surviving an earthquake seems to have made Mr Henry light-hearted, or perhaps it's relief, but what he's saying reminds me of a conversation between my father and Mr Henry, when they first talked about my coming here.

'There is no way we can catch the birds and release them without the help of man's best friend,' he explained. 'It requires patience to train one, but the success or failure of our kākāpō and kiwi rescues will depend on the dog – and Lassie is exceptional.'

He was right. Lassie is exceptional. Exceptional in the hunting sense but also exceptional in the personality sense. She is my friend. I would be even more lonely without her.

But *patience*! Mr Henry should have said *trouble*! Sure, he taught her to find, track and capture birds when they lived in Te Anau but perhaps this long, long waiting period has made her too eager and that was why she killed the weka family when we got here.

Since then we've caught another pair and put them where the first ones were, feeding them to encourage them to stay. Mr Henry has used the new weka to train Lassie not to give chase unless he commands her to. But to ensure there are no accidents, Mr *Dog-Discipline* Henry continues to make her wear a muzzle every day.

Lassie ready for work (c.1900) [1]

Yes, it's easy to love Lassie, she is the good part of my life here.

Then there's the other part of my life here. What I'm doing today. I simply can't believe I'm doing it.

Today we're searching for penguin eggs.

'They are plentiful and with a concern for future food we must gather them now, before the chicks start to form inside,' says Mr Henry.

'We're going to *eat* them!'

'No different from eating duck eggs, or quail eggs in England, Andy lad. When I was a boy in Australia,

I saw aboriginal people eat snake eggs. Crofters on the Scottish islands climb cliffs above savage seas to secure the eggs of all sorts of seabirds.'

I suppose he's right. I suppose wandering through a penguin colony is easy in comparison. But eating penguin eggs!

'We will preserve some of them now, to eat later in the year when the young have hatched and they're not laying eggs,' he says. 'We'll have to keep them away from the rats, though. Rats love eggs. Choose eggs not yet dirty, it's a sign they are fresh.'

How does he know these things?

Lassie comes with us of course.

Next thing? We head off to where there are hundreds of birds, which nest not far from each other in hollows under trees, rocks, or forest undergrowth. They make a rippling call when they see us but we move quietly, without sudden movements, and start to sneakily remove the cleanest eggs and put them in our buckets.

It's hopeless: even though Mr Henry hasn't given her a command, Lassie begins racing about and, using her head and shoulders, starts jostling the penguins, pushing them over. She can't bite them because of the muzzle but she won't let them stand up and roughly shoves and harms them. Chaos. Noisy, rushing chaos. The confused birds make shraak-shraak-shraak alarm calls. They charge here, there, squirting poo and falling over in anxiety. A few try to stay on their nests, as if to protect them. Feathers fly. Eggs break. Penguins fall. The more the penguins panic, the more excited Lassie gets; the more attacking she does, the more the penguins panic. The noise of their shraak-shraak-shraak mixed with other, high pitched, harsh trilling is overwhelming on top of their urgent squawks and loud screeches.

Pandemonium: noise, feathers, frantic movement.

Mr Henry leaps towards Lassie, gesturing with his arms. 'Lassie! Lassie! No! No! No! Sit! Confound you! Lassie! Sit dog, sit!'

Lassie is so busy she doesn't notice him for a few minutes but when she does, sits immediately. She is a *very* obedient dog. She also has the most expressive face. I can see her disappointment. She thought she was *helping.*

The birds continue charging all over the place, still making their raucous noises. Mr Henry tells off Lassie. He makes it clear she is a bad dog who has disgraced herself and he is angry with her. Then he tells me to continue collecting enough eggs to fill both buckets and takes her away from the penguins. I'm left on my own among these squawking, smelly, pooing birds to collect their eggs for *eating.* Lassie has her tail between her legs and slinks along beside Mr Henry. Mr Henry is angry. I don't like Mr *Mean-to-Lassie* Henry. I don't like this job. I don't like penguin eggs. I don't like this place. I want to go back to Dunedin.

Today we're on our way to Shelter Cove, which is

on the mainland. The penguin disaster is behind us and as usual Lassie is sitting up, very straight, in the prow of *Pūtangi*. She's looking eagerly ahead as a light northerly breeze tickles her coat and makes her spaniel ears flap a little. Her posture seems regal.

'Lassie, Lady of the Loch,' says Mr Henry. 'You could mistake her for a figurehead.' While I row – the wind is too light to be much use for sailing – he's coiling the anchor rope and looking at her fondly.

'She is important,' I say. 'And she knows it.'

'Yes. Best of all, today she can run down as many birds as possible. Run them down to her heart's content. She'll have a cracker of a day, helping with counting – and it will be interesting to see if she catches any stoats on the mainland.' I still haven't seen a live stoat, though Mr Henry has pointed out skat, and shells – which he says is evidence they are on the mainland and have been taking eggs.

We inspected Shelter Cove when we were checking the whole fiord at the beginning of our stay and it has a good landing site with an excellent camping spot beside a swift little stream of sweet water. Today we are not going to be actually *catching* the birds, but we are going to do a count of them: how many roa? How many kiwi? How many kākāpō? It may also be how many stoats or weasels. Anyway, at least it's a start.

Mr Henry has been explaining that we need to know this because, no matter how good the landing is, or the tent site, it won't be worth setting up a bird-catching camp when the time comes to do so unless there are plenty of birds nearby. Lassie loves all trips on the *Pūtangi* and likes sitting at the front of the boat. Sometimes dolphins join us and if that happens she gets ecstatic, barking and leaning out over the water as they leap in front of the boat and make a whooshing sound expelling air. There aren't any dolphins today but she is still happy in her position.

We get to Shelter Cove, pull up *Pūtangi,* secure the

grapnel well above the leaves, twigs and dry seaweed of the high-tide line and set off. We aren't carrying much – our billhooks of course, there's bound to be thick undergrowth, a swag so we can boil the billy for tea, the oilskin jackets, spare laces and dry socks we always carry. It's not raining. Lassie is her inquisitive, friendly, nosey, self: fossicking here, searching there, investigating this, sniffing that. There isn't much undergrowth and we walk among soft ferns as we go up and down gullies with the sweet, moist bush smell everywhere. We walk for a long time without success. We turn at the top of a ridge and head down a small valley when –

'What! Heavens! Mr Henry! Look at this!' I'm calling out with pleasure because, almost under my foot, is a kākāpō. I nearly *stood* on our first bird of the day. It's hiding half under and alongside a fallen log in a soft, mossy clearing. It doesn't make a sound.

This is the first time I've been right beside one; usually Lassie just disturbs a bird and Mr Henry adds it to his tally of 'numbers sighted: kiwi, roa, kākāpō' and we move off. This one must have frozen in the nearest available cover when it heard us coming and now, even though we are close and looking at it, it remains motionless. Lassie seems happy to leave it where it is and moves away, but I stay looking at it for a while. Everything about it is interesting.

The first thing I notice is its colour. Actually, that's not completely true. It is easy to *not* notice them because of their colour. Kākāpō are the same colours as their surroundings and as a result are perfectly camouflaged. Their plumage is a mix of the fern-green, punga-brown, moss-russet, leaf-amber, rain-grey, sunlight-gold, but every single feather contains a variety of those colours, mingled, dappled, flecked. Their habit of keeping still and blending into their surroundings would have been a good survival trick when the giant eagles and hawks flew above, looking for prey. Then, when they realise you only want to look at them, they peer back at you with dark, watchful eyes in round faces and

Kākāpō

It does not fly, but is an agile climber, and lives on mountains, high areas and river flats up to the scrub line.

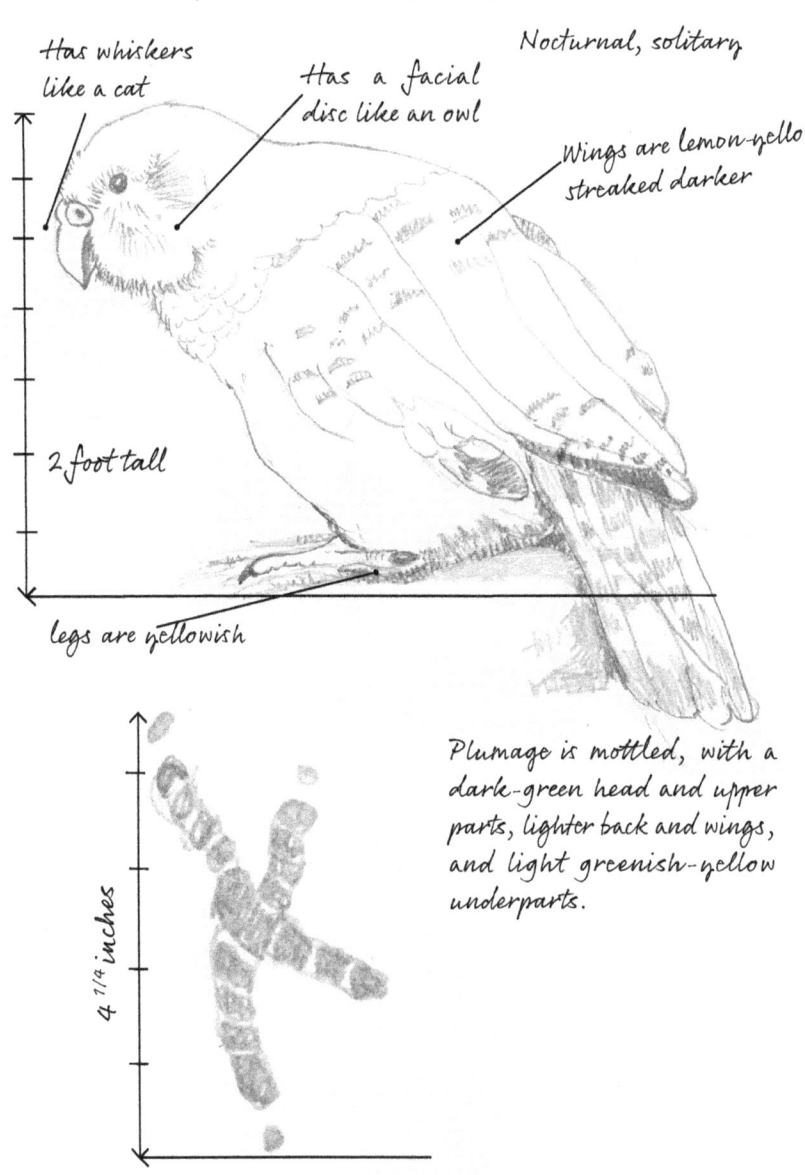

Has whiskers like a cat

Has a facial disc like an owl

Nocturnal, solitary

Wings are lemon-yellow, streaked darker

2 foot tall

legs are yellowish

4 1/4 inches

Plumage is mottled, with a dark-green head and upper parts, lighter back and wings, and light greenish-yellow underparts.

have a surprised but disapproving expression, as if to say *excuse me, I didn't invite you here and I don't want to chat, so please leave me alone.*

The other thing is their amazing feet which are as good as hands at holding onto things. Mr Henry says they don't peck you but can really kick with those feet, which they use to sort of 'run' up trees, using their wings for balance. The wings are of no use for flying but sometimes they almost spill themselves out of trees and then it's as if they are bouncing down a trunk or from a branch, and the stumpy wings help direct their way. The strangest thing about them is their scent. Most birds pong pretty bad – think of those penguins the other day, reeking of rotten fish and bird poo – but kākāpō have a lovely, fusty-warm smell that makes me think of horses and straw and oats in a stable. I have only been close enough to smell them a couple of times but I like the idea of being close to them when I catch them, and smelling them.

'If there's one here, there will be others in the vicinity, I'm positive,' says Mr *Hopeful* Henry. 'Wayo, Lassie, flush 'em out. Wayo.'

Lassie looks at him happily and wags her tail.

'Lassie, wayo, wayo,' says Mr Henry, making big, sweeping gestures at the surrounding bush. He does it a couple of times before Lassie gets the idea and leaves. 'That is strange, she usually bounds away at "wayo",' he says to me, adding, 'About time to boil the billy. We can have a brew in this nice spot and wait and see if Lassie rounds up another kākāpō or two.'

The tea is made and I'm pouring it into our enamel mugs when Lassie comes back. She isn't muddy or panting. It's obvious she hasn't been chasing anything. She looks happy enough and wags her tail when she sees us, then sits politely on dry moss, front feet straight and body held erect, as we sit quietly drinking our tea and eating yesterday's hard sultana scones. We're just about to put the mugs in the swag when a kākāpō walks straight into our clearing. We both see it at the same time and stay absolutely still, hardly daring to breathe. These birds don't have great eyesight and it seems unaware of our presence. What will it do when it sees us? I glance over at Lassie.

Lassie does nothing! She simply looks at the bird, not moving the tiniest muscle. We're astounded.

'Oi, Lassie!' says Mr Henry quietly. 'Oi. Catch!' Lassie looks at him, and raises her chin as if to say *I hear you but you can't confuse me with your tricks, Boss*, and continues to sit and do nothing. Mr Henry tries to get her to approach the bird by pointing to it but she won't make any movement. He goes to grab her by the collar and take her over to the bird but as soon as he makes a movement the bird scuttles quickly away. Lassie stays where she is.

This is unbelievable. *Any* dog gives chase at the sight of *anything* running away, it's instinct. And Lassie is more than *any* dog. Lassie always gives chase, we have never needed to tell her twice. Look at the way her instinct made her kill the weka, hunt the penguins, hunt for other kiwi and kākāpō.

But that explains one thing. That explains why there *seems* to be so few birds in the area. The birds are probably here but Lassie hasn't been hunting for them.

We turn back the way we came and walk to the boat in silence. Lassie seems to pick up on our subdued mood for she trots quietly two paces behind us both. We sail to the camp almost without speaking – which is not unusual with Mr *Don't-Waste-Words* Henry.

Lassie sits low in the boat, not in her usual place. She senses the atmosphere, I suppose. We get home. I boil potatoes, and open tinned bully beef for dinner. I feed Lassie. There's nothing to say.

'I think I know the cause of the problem.' Mr *No-Chat* Henry finally speaks after dinner. 'She must have decided she can't distinguish between different birds so, to play safe, won't take notice of any.'

'I can see why she'd think that.'

'I am at fault here. I have confused her.'

'So what will we do?' I ask.

'Well if I'm right, then we have two big problems on our hands. First of all, it means we can't be sure about bird numbers. Decisions about where to catch them, and how many to catch, depend on that information. The information we have collected so far cannot be trusted if Lassie has not been flushing them out for us. We may have to start our counting expeditions again.'

More delay until we start catching birds. I really *can't* stand more delay.

'And the other problem?' I ask.

'The other problem is worse: how will we find birds if Lassie won't?'

Lassie is sitting quietly beside Mr Henry. I lean over and give her a big hug. She's such a good dog and trying her best to do what she thinks we want her to do.

'She is here for a reason. If she cannot do the work we will have to get another dog,' says Mr *Logical* Henry. His words sound firm but I see his hand go out and he chucks her under the chin. 'Oh Lassie, Lassie, my girl, I am sorry if I have confused you,' he says softly. The broken tone of his voice tells me he doesn't trust himself to say any more.

If he gets another dog, what will happen to Lassie? I give her another hug. My eyes are watering. It's no fun here. Perhaps Lassie and I should go back to Dunedin together. My sisters would love her. So would Arthur.

He can't send her away. I don't think I can put up with being here if we don't have Lassie.

CHAPTER FOUR

Date: October, 1894

Bird tally: 0

Injuries tally: 3

- *Squashed little finger, left hand, caught between rock and Pūtangi when launching her, which matches my left-hand thumb, hit by hammer when holding a nail.*
- *My face and wrists and the backs of my hands, my neck – even my scalp – are one big injury; they are covered in sandfly bites and a lot of them are infected. This place is straight-out dangerous.*
- *A burn on my right hand from the camp oven when I was trying to make bread (very sore at first – and the bread wasn't like we have at home).*

This is what's been happening:

The *Hinemoa* is here! We're eating fresh mutton and apples and baker's bread and butter and there is even milk, which they picked up from Bluff! Baker's bread is white and soft and squashy and delicious, the stuff we make here doesn't even deserve the same name! I am eating it with real butter, not tinned butter, and it is like being in heaven. I know now what people mean when they talk about feasts and feasting. I could eat forever.

Mother has sent me chocolate. Chocolate!

Also there are letters from home, newspapers, and lots of people to talk to. It's as if the real, live world has come to Dusky Sound and everything that we have been doing here on our own has been unreal. Lassie loves the excitement and is leaping around and running from one sailor to another. Everybody likes her and pats her and says what a good dog she is. There is so much action and so much noise after the quietness we are used to.

There is so much delicious food!

I notice Mr Henry is looking happy, and that makes me wonder if he has been lonesome, too, just hasn't said so. Mr *Lonely* Henry is not a name I had thought of, but I notice how he pleased he is to get the papers and how he likes talking to the crew, who tell us what's been happening in the rest of the world. It's a strange feeling to realise how everything carries on as usual, even though we know nothing about it. Even at home the girls have been going to school and know about news and events I'm ignorant of.

'It's a time of change, lad,' one of the sailors says to me when I manage to get a quick look at a newspaper he offers Mr Henry. 'With the new laws, men don't have to work as long each day. Some are arguing we should only work for five days of each week. Imagine that! Two days to do as you please! And look at that!'

He makes a sort of squeaky sound and his stubby finger points at a picture of a woman in a large hat. 'See her, she's saying women, now they've got the vote – and that may still prove to be a dangerous thing – she is saying now they've got the vote, they should be allowed stand for Parliament. Women – in the government!'

My mother would agree with the woman in the hat. She reckons my four younger sisters should have the same education and rights four more sons would have had. I think perhaps I should ask him what would be wrong with women going to Wellington and deciding about laws but before I say anything another sailor speaks.

'Next thing they'll be wanting to wear our clothes and do our jobs, that's the truth,' he says. 'Terrible it is.'

I look at his clothes, which are dirty and need patching; at his hands, which are calloused from hauling ropes. I don't think many women will want his job but when others mutter agreement, I don't mention my mother's ideas – or his clothes and hands.

It cuts both ways, though. We might not know what's going on in the rest of the country, but they don't know about what happened here.

'We had a really scary earthquake last week,' I say. 'Have you heard?'

They haven't. At last, the chance to tell someone about what happened and how frightening it was and how I could have died.

'The noise was the worst part. It was so loud, like the train coming through the Port Chalmers tunnel, but much louder, like thunder. I thought the end of the world was coming.' I want to describe the overpowering sound, the trees moving, as if going somewhere, the ground swaying and jumping, the landslide, and then the sight of *Pūtangi* up the tree, and when we got back how our stacks of roofing iron and timber had moved.

'An earthquake, you say. I have heard of them, to be sure,' one replies but none of them seem interested.

'You wouldn't like it,' I tell them. 'Everything seemed to be growling and snapping and even when we thought it had stopped there were more jolts and more noises.' I want to tell the sailors about the great gashes in the mountains where earth and trees had slipped and how the seawater was dull with earth and messy with trees. I want them to know we could have been killed but no one says anything back to me or asks questions. I suppose our earthquake is as unreal to them as Dunedin has become for me. The truth is, I realise, they are not interested. They are interested in our new weka from Cascade Cove and feed them bits and pieces of food. Piopio, the native thrush that sometimes calls around to see what we are up to, keeps well away, probably because of all the noise they make.

I go back for seconds of everything.

And I haven't even started my chocolate!

Mr Henry finishes eating but can't settle to enjoying conversation, he's in a rush to get his mail ready and to write request lists which the boat will take away tomorrow.

He has not been expecting the *Hinemoa* for another week and has no letters ready for his friends, nor

Piopio (native thrush)

It is about twice the size of the introduced thrush.
Seems unafraid of humans.
Omnivorous — eats worms, insects, spiders as well as fruit seeds, mosses and grass.
Beautiful call and good at imitating other birds.

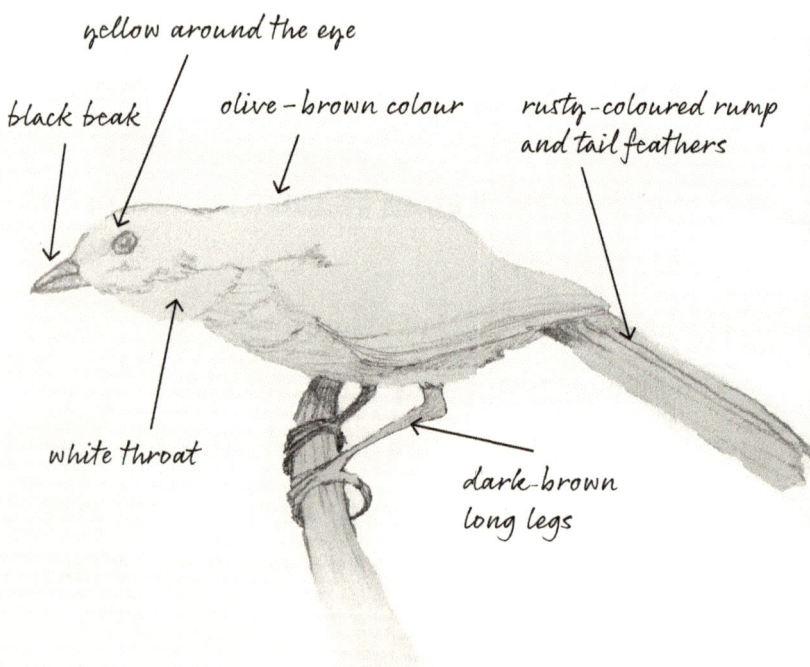

- yellow around the eye
- black beak
- olive-brown colour
- rusty-coloured rump and tail feathers
- white throat
- dark-brown long legs

Parents fake injury to lure predators away from their young.

finished his report for Mr Maitland, who's his boss. I'm the same – the letters I write are also too short and rushed.

Arthur didn't write but all my family did and asked lots of questions. I have only enough time to scrawl replies. I'll prepare better ones well before the boat next returns.

I thank Mother for the chocolate and tell her she can send me as much as she likes, as often as she likes. *You would enjoy the fish we catch to eat here,* I tell her. *They practically jump onto our hooks. Mr Henry says we will try and get crayfish when it is warmer. We have cleared trees and planted a vegetable garden. So far the carrots and silver beet and beans are all doing well – we even ate rhubarb last week.*

My next letter will describe what Mr Henry has taught me to cook. I'm keeping that in reserve as it will really surprise her. *Fiordland weather is as you said it would be. Rain or drizzle or damp, misty air mostly. You were right to insist I bring warm blankets, and thank you, too, Mother, for my oiled jacket and trousers. It would be unbearable without them.*

You should see the dolphins! I write to my sisters. *The jumping and splashing they make when they come around our part of Dusky Sound, I reckon they leap up just for fun. And every dawn the birds are so noisy they wake me up.* I tell them how Lassie killed Mr Henry's tame weka when we arrived and I add *I wish you could see the new weka we have caught, the ones the sailors like so much, which we have named Scrag and Yellow. They're very tame now, hang about where we pull the boat up, and beg for scraps of food all the time.*

I write an extra note to Victoria: *We eat penguin eggs, and I have to dig ashes and fish guts into the rhubarb and vegetable garden.* She loves disgusting stuff. *Dear Nancy,* I write, *there used to be sealers here but they have killed nearly every single seal and*

Mr Henry says that could happen to the roa, kiwi and kākāpō. Nancy has a soft heart.

I write to the little ones. *Dear twins, here are some feathers for you. The red ones are from kākā, grey from kiwi, brown from roa, white from the tui's throat, navy from wood pigeon, green from kākāpō.*

I wish I could get a little tin and put the warm smell of kākāpō in it and send it to them so they could take the tin to bed and take little whiffs as they drop off to sleep. I'd like them to know the old and comfortable smell of kākāpō, making you feel as if they were part of your life from before you were even born. And the twins would love Piopio, which comes inside our camp and looks around as if to say *So, what are you doing here, exactly? And what have you got for me to examine?* They would be so amused if they saw how it perches on the edge of Mr Henry's enamel mug to sip at his tea, and how it sings to itself in the small mirror we have.

Then the first light of morning comes, the crew

unload a few more supplies overlooked last night – extra nails, kerosene for the lamp, things like that – and collect our letters. In no time at all the boat pulls up its anchor and heads towards Five Fingers Peninsula. It gives a hoot as it nears the point.

They are gone.

We are on our own again.

After all the noise and conversation of last night it seems very quiet. Even Lassie looks dejected – or maybe she is tired from all the excitement.

'It is unfortunate we were not prepared for them,' Mr Henry says as the boat disappears round the headland. 'The Commissioner requires me to diary where we go, what we see, and to describe Resolution Island. It was a very slapdash report – but I did tell him how I failed to muzzle the dog when we arrived and how she killed the weka and the penguins.'

I'm surprised at Mr Henry openly admitting he'd made a mistake but remember Father saying one reason he would allow me to come was because Mr Henry is 'one of nature's gentlemen and as honest as they come'. Father didn't know Mr Henry hardly ever talks, his jokes aren't very funny, is a slave driver, and in no rush to catch birds.

'Did you tell him how Lassie won't chase anything now and we've ordered a new dog?' I ask.

Mr Henry sighs. I must admit he loves Lassie as much as me.

'I did.'

'Did you tell him we haven't captured any birds yet?'

'I did. And I told him they are plentiful on the mainland.'

'Did you tell him when we will start?'

'I know you are itching to get onto the catching, Andy lad, but we need to do things one at a time. If we cannot look after ourselves, we will hardly be able to look after the birds.' Mr *No-Rush* Henry speaks quietly but firmly.

I wish he were saying something else.

'Besides, we must wait for the *Hinemoa* to bring the new dog on her next visit.'

'And then how long will it take to train it?' I ask, kicking a nearby log in frustration, seeing more and more weeks go by, wondering if we will ever get started on our real task.

Mr Henry is quiet now. I suppose he's remembering all the time and love he put into training Lassie and how proud of her he has been.

Another thing Father said was you can tell a man's worth, not by what he says he's done or says he'll do, but by his attitude to what he has done or will do. Mr Henry's attitude is careful planning and quiet determination so no doubt we will eventually catch lots of birds, get them off the mainland and onto Resolution Island, save them from stoats, weasels, ferrets.

Eventually, I – we – will be famous.

The visit of the *Hinemoa* taught me something. I've been miserable because of the rats and the sandflies and the food and the delays. I became really miserable at the thought of Lassie being sent back to Dunedin and I wanted to leave and go with her. But after reading the papers, and despite getting letters from home, I realise I'm not so keen to go back. This place is starting to be all right. I like sailing and rowing. I like learning to make tracks and how to build. I like learning the names and habits of birds and the names of trees. I like the bush and the water and the silence. I like being 'Chief Assistant to the Chief Conservator', who, after all, is only sometimes a slave driver. One day we will be in the papers. I want to stay here until our work is finished and we are famous.

CHAPTER FIVE

Date: December, 1894 – March, 1895

Bird tally: 0

Injuries tally: Uncountable,

- *Sandfly bites. Huge, hundreds and hurting. In fact maybe thousands of them, like erupting volcanos on every part of my body.*
- *Blisters on both hands from rowing and from cutting tracks with the billhooks were bad enough but now I have them from bush felling because Mr Henry wants to plant a plot of grass here for sheep and goats, and for pūtangitangi, which most people call paradise ducks. They are his favourite birds, which is why he called his boat* Pūtangi.

This is what's been happening:

It's December and we can hear kākāpō drumming.

Pūtangitangi
(Paradise Ducks)

Easy to recognise because the female has a white head. The male has more subtle tones of chestnut, brown and black. They eat pond plants and aquatic insects.

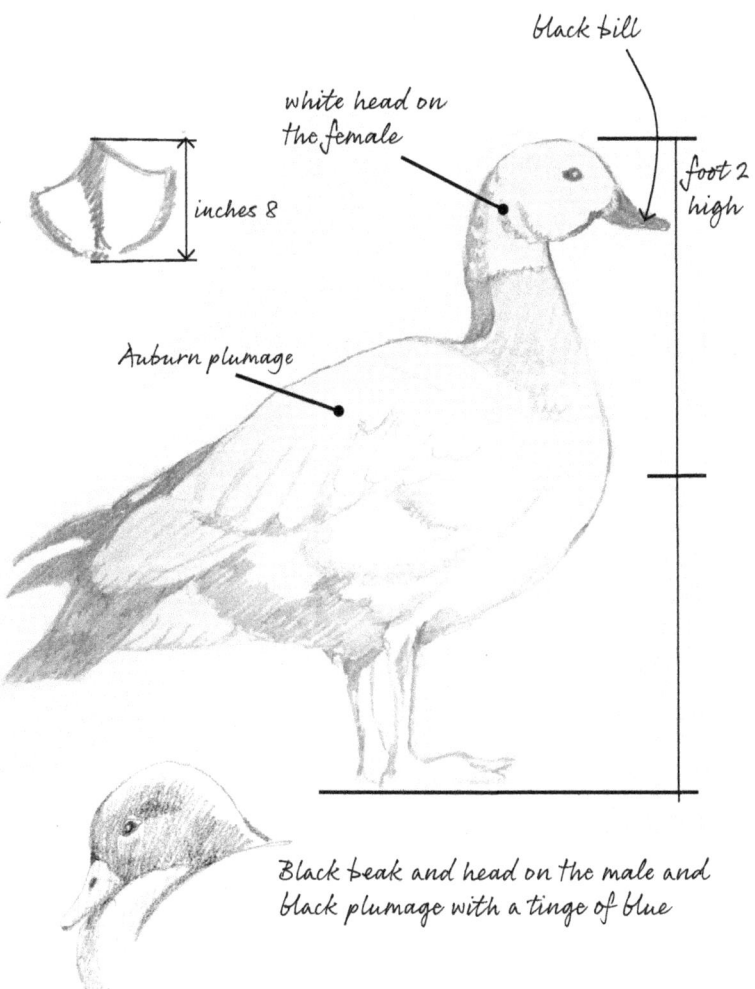

inches 8

black bill

white head on the female

foot 2 high

Auburn plumage

Black beak and head on the male and black plumage with a tinge of blue

Hhrumm ... hhrumm ... hhrumm ... hhrumm ... hhrumm

It is the eeriest noise.

They start with deep grunts and this turns into an eerie, very low, deep, booming throb. The hills reverberate with the noise: hhrumm ... hhrumm ... hhrumm ... which continues all night long so the pulsing sound seems to be part of the heaving water, the bush with its secrets, the hunkered-down islands and impassive mountains. It's as if the whole fiord is thrumming to itself – and then the echo is thrumming back on itself.

Mr Henry thinks he knows how they do it.

'When I was in Te Anau I found little tracks, like sheep tracks, along the tops of ridges. They were about this wide,' he holds his hands at almost the width of his shoulders, 'and about fifty yards long. Males would trim off any leaves leaning over the sides of their track, then create nice round holes on it by using their beaks to loosen soil and their feet to scoop it out. They'd settle themselves into the holes and utter their booms – the bowl shape seems to magnify the sound and project it.'

'Do they boom to attract a mate?'

'Most probably – I suppose the best boomer wins the most beautiful female.' He chuckles. Sometimes he can be almost chatty.

'You're sure it is kākāpō that make the tracks and do the booming?' I ask. This is another thing making them unique, everything about these birds is amazing, how they move, what they do, what they look like, their perfume.

'Oh yes. Their droppings were scattered all around – sometimes purple from eating tutu berries.' He chuckles again. 'They can be a bit messy. I've even seen them with purple tutu juice stains on their front feathers, like a grubby child.'

'So, do they just open their mouths and out comes the noise?'

'They puff up their throat with air – making their

chests looked huge, give a few grunts and release the air in little spurts,' says Mr Henry, 'which reverberate like a drum.'

Maybe that is why they always look a bit baffled and surprised – maybe they are surprised at their own selves, and the noise they hear themselves making. I'm becoming more familiar with them from our counting expeditions, but I can never tell what they're thinking. Often their eyes have a faraway expression, as if they have woken from a dream and would like to go back to it. I've come to expect them to stay very still, blending into the background, but know that if I try to touch them they scoot off, disappearing into the mossy, leafy, ferns and roots.

'And this forever drizzle doesn't worry them?' I ask.

'Seems not. And with the amount of drumming they're doing I think this will be a cracker year with lots of baby kākāpō.'

Well the never-ending drizzle may not worry them,

but I hate the way we have to put up with it. A decent storm will pass through and you can get on with things again. Not the drizzle. It's like the air itself is seeping damp. Everything is an oozing wetness which collects into drips. If you look up, they drop off your hat brim and down the back of your neck. If you look down, they fall onto your nose and then down the front of your neck. Beads of water drip off ferns and into your boots. The drizzle goes on and on and you have no idea how long it will last and even wonder if it will end at all. It's not bad enough to stay inside the tent as we do when a stormy southerly blows, but it is bad enough to make every single thing we do miserable. Forget anything I've said before: this really is an awful place.

And we are still not catching birds.

It's February. The *Hinemoa* came and went last month – and brought our new dog. Mr Henry ordered a fox terrier because it's a breed which loves to hunt small animals – and it turns out fox terriers love to hunt birds, too. He's really quick and has already learned he may only hunt if he's wearing the muzzle, but if it's not on, he can't so much as *look* at a bird. He's been practising on weka, ducks and penguins and is a great finder.

But I feel so sorry for Lassie.

When we started training Foxy we tethered Lassie at home, but the sandflies attacked her ferociously and, being tied up, she couldn't get away from them. We take her with us now but it breaks her heart when she sees how we make a fuss of Foxy when he finds a bird – and it's breaking our hearts to see her broken heart! She doesn't understand why Foxy is allowed to hunt when she was punished for it. Mr Henry had hoped she might learn from him or imitate him, but she hasn't. It's because she is obedient: she has got it into her head that she must not chase any bird, ever, so she doesn't.

'I'll send her back to my friend Melland when the

Hinemoa next calls,' he says. 'He looked after her once before, when I left Te Anau to go to Auckland.'

I can't say a word. Lassie! Banished!

It's March and I am on the shore by *Pūtangi*. I'm giving Scrag and Yellow cabbage stalks and stale damper and waiting for Mr Henry to come down the track from the tent-hut and say where we'll go counting today. The weka are funny – they spend most of their time fossicking for sandhoppers and anything else they can find on the beach, but the moment they see me they rush up, hoping for food. And of course, I always find something to give them; they are noisy, bossy, demanding – and comical.

Mr Henry arrives. 'It's a good day to start constructing the foundations for our permanent home.'

'What!' I almost shout the words. 'What?' I repeat. I don't want to hear what he's saying. I feel my anger rising.

'We've checked all the bays and islands, and I've quite decided none of them can compete with what we have here on Pigeon Island, so this is where we'll build the house.'

'Build the house! What do you mean "build the house?!"' I do shout now.

'It's time to be making a start on it. After we've built the house and a boatshed, we can extend the garden you've worked on and make it permanent.'

I feel my anger turning to rage. I kick a stone near my foot but I really want to kick his foundations. Kick his timber. Kick his roofing iron. Kick his garden most of all.

'But Sir!' I can't help shouting. 'We now have a trained dog. We know our way round Dusky Sound. We have checked where there are plenty of different birds. We have cut tracks over Resolution Island.' I stomp three paces away from him and the boat and pause in an effort to stop shouting. Then I turn back and speak very slowly. 'We are all right in our canvas hut. We have established a garden. I have cleared bush and sown grass. I came here to –'

I choke a bit then and can't say any more. I'm too old to cry but not too old to feel like crying.

'What's upsetting you, Andy lad?'

'Why can't we start catching birds?' I stand straight and glare straight at him. I put my shoulders back. It's time we had this out.

'I. Came. Here. To. Catch. Birds. It's the only reason we're here. To. Catch. Birds. Why are you talking about starting to build the house now?' I grab a bit of driftwood near my feet and use both hands to hurl it as far as I can onto the water.

Mr Henry takes his eyes from my face and follows the trajectory of the driftwood. He turns back to me and speaks slowly.

'Think, Andy. While we've been training Foxy he's found kākāpō babies and young kiwi. If we capture birds now, we may be taking them from their young ones, which would then starve to death. We'll have to wait until all the young have fledged.'

I want to break something in frustration.

Will we only ever count birds and never capture and save them? Will I spend the rest of my time here in this drip, drip, dripping drizzle, being eaten by bloodthirsty sandflies, saving our food and supplies from voracious rats, cooking and building and gardening and cutting down trees? (I'm not even mentioning penguin eggs.)

If Arthur were here we could run away. Right now I'm sick of this place and sick of this life. I know Mr Henry is right – but that only makes everything worse.

It's still March and we're building the house. It's good to learn to build and Piopio likes to supervise, flying about as we raise beams and nail boards. He loves it when I disturb spiders – he eats almost everything but *loves* spiders. The house is going to have two bedrooms, which is good because Mr Henry snores loudly.

'There will be one big main room, with a tub

for washing, a fireplace for cooking, a bench and cupboards and shelves,' Mr Henry says. He reckons he can make a table and chairs, too.

When I'm not working on the house, I spend time forming steps on the track from the house down to the shore where we'll build a boat shed after we finish the house. When I finish the steps Mr *Crack-the-whip* Henry gives me a new job.

'We require a bigger garden. You'll need to collect guano and seaweed, crush up some shells to make lime and get ash from the fire. Dig all that in, then add any dead birds you come across and the guts, as well as heads and tails, from fish you catch. That will make the soil fertile.'

Is he trying to torture me?

I didn't come here to be a *gardener*. I could have been a gardener in Dunedin.

Also, talking about 'guano' makes it sound all right, but guano is actually bird poo: straight bird poo, nothing else. Shags eat fish all day, then roost together and poo it out all night. It builds up and can be scooped up with a shovel. I hate it. It is full of ammonia, making my eyes water and my nose feel funny – and the stink! Oh help, the stink! It gets worse: with my eyes streaming and nose running and holding my breath so I don't have to smell it too much I almost always meet a bird that decided to have a sleep-in and not go fishing. Of course it gets a fright when it sees me so the first thing it does is poo right in front of me. It feels like a deliberate insult.

And Mr *Guano-Torturer* Henry tells me when the garden's finished my next job will be to cut and clear part of the island so we can grow even more grass to attract paradise ducks. He became keen on them when he lived in Te Anau.

'You could be quietly riding along and you'd hear them make a call which meant "here comes a horseman", or they might see other ducks and cry "there are strange ducks coming".'

'They actually have a language?'

'Oh yes, Andy lad. They have a call for "beware there's a hawk" which is different from "let's fly away somewhere else".'

I'm not too concerned about what ducks say. I am concerned about chopping down trees, which means more blisters. So far he hasn't said I must put guano on the pūtangitangi paddocks, but he still might.

Kākāpō booming is not the only mystery here. Today when I was digging our garden I discovered heaps and heaps of shells which Mr Henry says means there will be old Māori ovens nearby. Did they live here, or just visit? What happened to them? Then I came across the remains of a path made from gravel and punga with broken china nearby. I asked him about that.

'Sealers perhaps, or shipwrecked sailors. Could have been escaped Australian convicts.' But Mr Henry doesn't really know. 'There were European people staying here long before anyone settled in

Northland because Dusky Sound is straight across from Sydney, Australia. And because Captain Cook had charted it all.'

We're doing building work, tree-felling work, digging-and-planting-a-garden work, collecting and spreading disgusting-guano work. Hard work.

But no birding.

It's April, the *Hinemoa* is making its three-monthly visit and has brought supplies and letters. It's taking away our letters and Mr Henry's reports.

The *Hinemoa* is also taking Lassie.

I think my heart will break as I say goodbye to her. She's tethered on the ship and sees me get down into *Pūtangi* without her. She looks and looks at me but doesn't make a movement or a sound, not even a whimper. She looks and looks. Obedient, tail-wagging Lassie. There will never be a dog as good as Lassie. She *understands* things. She knows when I'm miserable. She has a little way of pushing her nose into my hand when she thinks I'm lonely. Sometimes, when the dolphins came in and leaped out of the water, huffing and splashing and we ran down to jump from rock to rock alongside them, shouting and laughing back, she would look at me with such mischief in her eyes, as if to say, *They think we're both people, they don't know I'm a dog, isn't that a funny thing!*

Tricky, funny Lassie. At dinner time she'd sometimes sit very straight with her head on one side, staring at me, and I knew what she was thinking: *Well he's not going to give me any more dog dinner but if I look really earnest and appealing perhaps he will give a little bit off the side of his plate.* Then one ear would flop over and she'd give me a cute look. And, yes, I would give her a little bit off the side of my plate.

But it wasn't just about food. She would tease me when I carved a ball from kelp stems. If I threw it she would catch and drop it one step away from me, then as soon as I moved towards it, she would lunge away with the ball, to drop it two paces away. If I moved towards it again, she would leap in front and snatch it away. She was laughing at me – laughing in a dog way, you could see it in her eyes. She loved playing that game.

It is arranged she'll go to Mr Henry's friend, Mr Melland. Mr *Dog-Banisher* Henry is sad, too, as he says goodbye. He says she will have a happy life at Mr Melland's big Te Anau sheep run, where she can chase as many pūkeko and ducks as she likes and there won't be any muzzles. I think Mr Henry was trying to convince himself as well as me.

Nothing is turning out the way I hoped or expected. We spend a lot of time talking about Lassie now she's gone. It helps us both to do so. We miss everything about her – even the way she showered us when she shook her curly coat to get rid of water after she had been in the sea. We remember the way she would almost dance with impatience as she waited for Mr Henry to say 'wayo'. We talk about her trying to hide under the seat in *Pūtangi* the first time a whale blew right beside us.

I don't dislike Foxy. He is very determined and also likes to play. Actually, he is a very good little dog. It's not his fault Lassie had to leave.

There is another change: at nights, after Mr Henry has finished writing his notes, he makes cages we will use when transporting birds. I watch him sawing and then chiselling, planing, sandpapering. I hear the tap, tap, as he fits the pieces of dowel and wood together and sometimes he sighs a little as he works. It's not like the evenings I remember at home. My sisters would chat and sing as they drew or embroidered while Mother darned stockings. They would tease each other – and often me, too. It was a warm feeling.

Mr *No-Chat* Henry doesn't talk while he is making the cages. Foxy is a good and willing little dog but he can't talk. Arthur is miles and miles away. Lassie …

I'm not going to think about this lonely life. The cages have handles and when on a birding expedition we will use them to carry the birds from the bush where we catch them to the camps where we stay. We will also use them when we take them on *Pūtangi* from our camping places to Resolution Island.

Mr Henry says we will start catching and rescuing birds in May.

It will be May next week.

CHAPTER SIX

Date: May, 1895
Bird tally: roa x 5; kiwi x 2; kākāpō x 6
Injuries tally: 0 (no serious ones anyway)
I hurt all over. I'm happy all over.

This is what's been happening:

'He's got something,' says Mr Henry.

I throw down the pack, grab the sugar bag and begin running like crazy up a steep, muddy gully towards the noise. As usual the bush is thick and hard to shove through and as I run low branches and looping kiekie vines slap and grab me. I lurch, trip, half fall. What has he found? A kākāpō? A kiwi? Will it get away? Faster. Forcing myself forward. Aiming for the sound of the barking dog and the clanging bell tied to his collar.

'Aaargh!' The sound heaves out of me as I slip,

slither down the bank I'd just clambered up, then slip again, landing on my side. Winded, I clutch at a houhere tree, and, like a bucket being emptied, huge drops of water fall from it and soak my clothes. I don't stop to catch my breath. Up and up I go, my shoulder still aching from the tōtara root I tripped over this morning, the lawyer vine scratches on my face and hands stinging. Young lancewoods sway nearby and I grip their spindly trunks.

'Foxy! Foxy!' I shout, frantic. The day before a kākāpō ran towards a waterfall and the noisy rushing water drowned the noise of the bell, so I nearly didn't find dog or bird. Foxy never, ever gives up. He'll toss and shove a bird – even to death. I must get there and grab the bird before the dog does any serious damage.

A lawyer vine catches the sugar bag, toppling me, and I slide over the top half of a large, mossy boulder. Panting, gasping for air, I lurch myself upright and keep climbing. I hardly notice any of this, all I feel is overwhelming panic. I must get to the bird. I must.

The dog barks again. I can hear the bell and it sounds close. I grab hold of a low beech branch and swing myself into a more open area of bush, where a dozen young rimu trees fight each other to reach the light. Yes! There is the dog! There is the bird! A big fat kākāpō, green-gold and solid, baled up in a hole formed by roots of a massive fallen rimu. A beauty of a bird! I throw the sugar bag over it, grab the covered bundle in my arms, pull it close to my chest, and shout at the dog.

'Good boy. Good. Quiet.' Foxy continues to jump and bark, his tail thrashing, the bell jangling.

'Quiet now. Sit. Sit.' The poor bird is dazed enough by the presence of the dog, let alone all the movement and noise. Foxy sits down nearby, salivating and pleased with himself. Somehow he manages to wag the end of his tail though he is sitting on it.

'Coo-ee. Coo-ee.' Australian style, I give a couple of loud calls, and listen for Mr Henry's returning shout, at the same time pressing the bundle firmly against my body. As soon as I hear an answering 'Coo-ee' I give my attention back to the bird. Its distinctive, musky smell, fuggy and rich, reminding me of my mother's fur coat and horses and stables and chalk and dust, is close, earthy and very strong. I sniff deeply. And again. I feel for its head beneath the covering of sacking, then manoeuvre the rest of the body into an upright position. The bird doesn't move or make a sound but I can feel the rapid beat of its heart and the heat of its body.

'Foxy. Sit.' He's whimpering and making movements towards the undergrowth but he isn't allowed to do any more hunting till Mr Henry's here and the kākāpō transferred to the cage. I wait, keeping the bird upright with its head covered, and then there's another 'Coo-ee,' which doesn't sound too far away. I answer it, then take more sniffs of kākāpō scent while I stand there. The bird is not struggling.

Foxy watches me as I wait. There is another call to

Tokoeka (common name southern brown kiwi)

Also called Roa.

A soft, shaggy bird, with whiskers. It has short legs, no tail and doesn't fly.

It eats worms and invertebrates and sometimes fallen fruit.

Mostly nocturnal and lives on tussock grassland, in scrub or native forest. The female is larger than the male which is about 20 inches high.

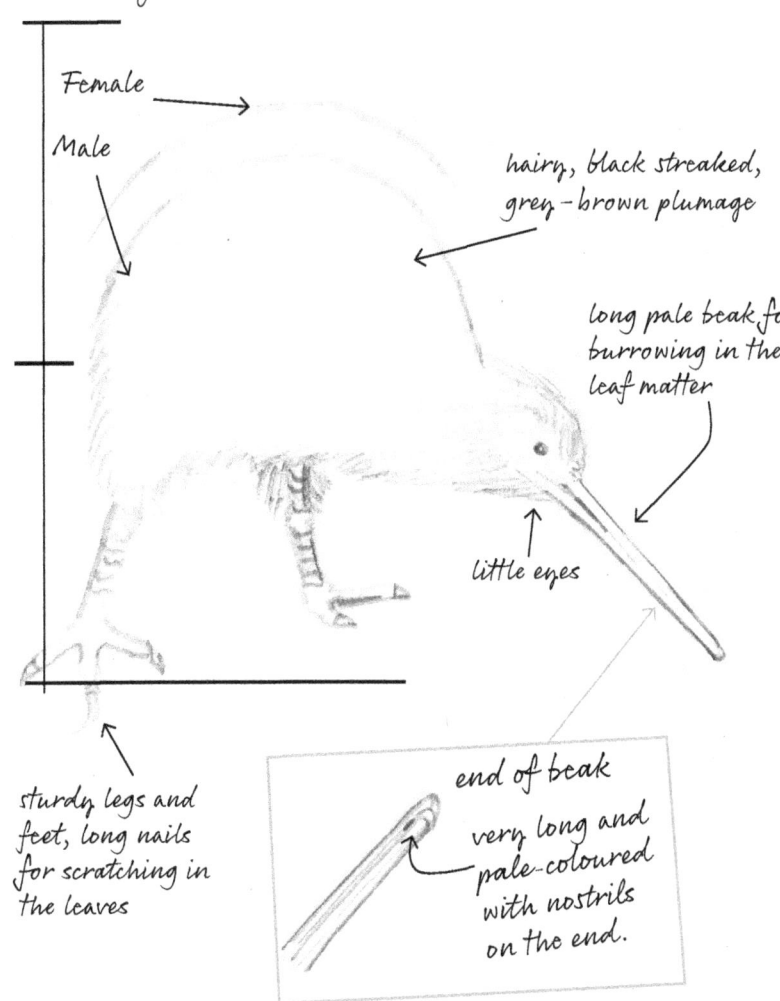

Female →
Male ↓

hairy, black streaked, grey-brown plumage

long pale beak for burrowing in the leaf matter

little eyes

sturdy legs and feet, long nails for scratching in the leaves

end of beak very long and pale-coloured with nostrils on the end.

answer before heavily laden Mr Henry lumbers in. He places the bulky equipment, including the cage from off his back, on the ground. He opens a section of the cage so it is ready for the bird and then very gently takes the kākāpō, still in its sugar bag wrapping, from me.

We don't speak. What he's doing is too important for us to be talking. Mr Henry turns the swaddled bird carefully, then gently loosens the material near its legs and examines its feet: the two front-pointing toes and two back-pointing ones on each yellowish leg appeared unharmed. He feels its body and wings through the sacking, then, still keeping its head covered, takes a surreptitious look at its trunk. No obvious sign of damage, its feathers, the colour of moss and beech leaves, are untidy and mussed but the yellow markings on its wings, showing it's a male, are clear.

'Well, what a cracker of a bird,' he says aloud, then drops his voice and speaks soothingly to it. 'You are a handsome fellow. Now don't fret, you'll be fine.'

Foxy looks at Mr Henry. He thumps his tail. He also wants attention. Mr Henry turns to him. 'Good boy, well done.' He gives me a little nod of his head.

I'm ready beside the open part of the cage. Mr Henry squats alongside and then, in one swift movement, he bundles the bird into it and I quickly slam the door and fasten it.

We both gaze at the bird, which is hunched and cautiously peering out: his whiskers, sprouting from each side of his beak and nostrils, are not damaged. His huge eyes, a little like an owl's, survey us solemnly. He must be puzzled by what's happened and must be afraid but makes no sound. The most important thing is that he's not hurt, and I can tell Mr Henry's pleased with what he's looking at.

'Good work all round,' he says. He means he's pleased with the dog, with my race to catch it, and with the bird itself.

'Yes,' he says. 'A fine, healthy male, nice and fat,

with shining feathers. A cracker of a bird, in his prime.' We both know the kākāpō will need his reserves of fat and energy over the next few days of captivity.

I pick up the cage, which already has a small grey-coloured kiwi in the first section, and slip its straps over my shoulders. Next time the dog finds a bird it will be Mr Henry's turn to drop anything he's holding to run, and it will be me who follows with the cage containing the kiwi and now a kākāpō, as well as the pack, billhook and other gear. Mr *Not-So-Bad-When-He's-Hunting-Kākāpō* Henry tells Foxy to track another bird.

'Way now Foxy, wayo,' he says, and we begin struggling up yet another steep rise.

Things I hate about Dusky Sound:
1) sandflies
2) rats
3) williwaws
4) sandflies
5) earthquakes
6) gardening
7) sandflies
8) penguin poo
9) Arthur not being here
10) sandflies

Things I love about Dusky Sound:
1) Lassie
2) Foxy
3) kākāpō
4) queen pudding
5) fluffy penguin omelettes
6) damper, sultanas and syrup
7) the 'chase'
8) Piopio drinking Mr Henry's tea
9) sailing Putangi in a light breeze
10) the quietness, the stillness

Five Fingers – Dusky Sound

Things the Hinemoa brings:
1) letters from home
2) chocolate
3) letters from Arthur
4) baker's bread
5) sailor's gossip
6) fresh beef & mutton
7) apples
8) cheese
9) The Otago Daily Times
10) fresh stores of whatever we have run out of: tins of butter or syrup, chests of tea or dried peas, bags of flour, sugar, or oatmeal

CHAPTER SEVEN

Date: June, 1895

Bird tally: roa x 15; kiwi x 7; kākāpō x 13

Injuries tally: Whatever part of me you can see is a complete mess. My face and neck and wrists and the backs of my hands are covered in scratches from branches that have slapped at me and vines that have grabbed at me and stones and rocks that have grazed me when I fall and there is no way you can tell what are sandfly bites and what is merely bush revenge. The other bits of me, the bits you can't see, are all different-coloured bruises from falls – purple and yellow and blue and brown.

But I don't care.

This is what's been happening:

I feel disloyal to Lassie.

But I have to admit Foxy's an excellent hunter,

probably as good as Lassie before she gave up chasing birds. He's finding lots.

We're going on a bird hunt again today but before we can set off we have to load *Pūtangi*. This takes ages because there are so many things we need to take. Lots of things means a heavily loaded boat, this means the boat sits very low in the water, this means it could tilt and capsize: this means I am very nervous.

Add to that, boating in this place is always scary because of the unpredictable weather. Have I mentioned that this boat has a small keel, so it is hard to row, hard to sail, and even harder to manoeuvre into coves? What's worse is that if a storm comes up and you need shelter in a hurry, landing places are scarce – in other words, very few and very far between.

There's quite enough to be scared about without overloading the boat.

Before we leave Mr *Organised* Henry calls out a list to make sure we've remembered everything.

'Sailing gear – anchor? sails? oars? lines? ropes?'

I say yes each time.

'Camping needs – tent and fly, bedding?'

'Yes.'

'Camp oven and billies, food?'

'Yes.'

'Dog muzzle, dog bell, spare muzzles, spare bells?'

'Yes.'

He continues as if he were reading from a list but the list's in his head. There's a lot of equipment to be stashed in boxes and tins to keep them dry: telescope, compass, charts, maps and notebooks, as well as baskets for fishing gear, net, lines and hooks. We stack them all in. He doesn't mention clothing but we each take an oilskin coat and leggings, undershirts and jackets, spare trousers and boots, several pairs of socks. Lastly there's Foxy, the backpack birdcage and the bird-transporting cages.

So that's why the boat sits low in the water, and that's why I'm nervous.

On our first expedition we discovered the cages Mr Henry made are good for transporting them to the island on the boat, but hopeless in the bush – too cumbersome. They needed one of us on each side to carry it, which is almost impossible amongst trees and gullies. Mr Henry thought about making a smaller one, but that would mean each time we caught a bird we would have to abandon the hunt to take it back to a big cage at camp, which would require hours of useless trudging back and forth through the bush. Then he came up with the idea of a backpack cage, which one of us would carry, leaving the other free to chase after the dog when it baled up a bird.

His new cage was a great success and I stow it carefully in the stern. Foxy loves everything. To him it's all an adventure, he sniffs at the cage while I'm carrying it and he jumps excitedly in and out of the boat, his tail flicking me sometimes as I stow the last of the gear.

He is a very good dog. He will never be Lassie.

Where we go depends on three things: how many birds we have previously seen in that area, how long it is since we were last collecting there, and always, always, always, the weather. It must be settled enough to sail there, then stay calm while we are camping and searching. When we have a load of birds, we still need calm weather while we take them from the camp to Resolution Island and release them, then sail or row back to our now mostly-built house on Pigeon Island. If the weather changes unexpectedly we must break camp early for fear of being stuck away from home with no food. It can take a week or more for a southerly spell to go through and we wouldn't easily survive that long without food, in a light tent.

We get to our chosen spot, beach *Pūtangi*, set up the tent and put everything into it. Packing, travelling and setting-up takes the whole day.
We start the day, as fresh and eager as Foxy, with

me carrying the backpack cage. We lose the first bird – if there was one. I have a feeling Foxy is so keen for action he might sometimes bark in the hope of frightening a bird out of hiding and earn praise that way.

I chase after the sound of his bell and listen for barking but when I catch up there is definitely no bird, and he looks sheepish, as if he knows he's been a bit optimistic.

We lose the next bird, too, I'm not sure what happens but I'm sure there is a real one this time: we hear Foxy bark, we hear the bell ring and Mr Henry gets straight onto the chase but when he finds Foxy, he is alone.

'He's looking embarrassed,' Mr Henry says when I lumber up, weighed down by the cage and gear, 'but there're no feathers around him. Perhaps he found something that could fly.' Foxy hates to lose his quarry – you can see that from his expression of hurt pride.

We devour lunch after all that activity. I've made sandwiches with tinned bully beef and mustard in slices of damper. For afters we have fruit cake Mr Henry made at the house. He says I'm not yet a good enough cook to risk wasting a lot of sultanas. We drink water from a stream. Believe me, you'd never die of thirst in Fiordland.

After lunch we start to slog up the nearby gully and it's again my turn to give chase. Foxy finds a bird nearby and though that means I don't have to do another one of those mad dashes, I still rush to him urgently.

If it's a kākāpō it will probably be bowed and turned into a ball-like shape to avoid him, but if it's a roa, it'll be slashing wildly with its strong legs and feet and could injure him. I was right to be worried.

'A roa,' I yell, though I know Mr Henry is unlikely to be able to hear me. 'And it's a huge one.'

It certainly is. A strong roa, which must be a female because it is so big, and does it put up a fight! I know it can hardly see me but it will be smelling me, smelling Foxy of course, and panicking. Its legs are not long but it lashes out, using vicious claws on the end of its toes and I'm glad I have an oilskin jacket covering me, though I don't want that ripped, either.

It's a frustrating struggle to get the burlap around the bird and when I eventually do, I have to hold it facing away from my body so it can't claw at me. I keep telling Foxy to quieten but he won't, making me pleased to see Mr Henry and the cage. We get the roa into it, yet Foxy keeps on barking at the hole it came from, with his bell ringing.

'Ah, of course!' says Mr Henry. 'There is another one in the hole. Cracker!'

He's right. There is another, a young one, in the gap between gnarled tree roots. We've caught two roa in less than an hour and are making up for the morning's poor results. We put it in the cage, too. We're doing what we came here to do – rescuing kiwi and kākāpō. I love the chase – love it. I know I said it was good I didn't have a big run for the last two captures, but actually there is nothing to beat that crazy, whooping race.

When I'm running for a bird, nothing else exists. There is only me, the noise of the dog and bell, and the urgency to get there. I don't think about the bush – or injuries – or Mr Henry. I didn't know anything could feel so exhilarating. From now on I will put up with any difficulty or danger – rats, sandflies, rain, earthquakes, guano, terrible weather, scary boating – *anything* – so I can live here and catch these special birds.

I realise Mr Henry has said something and is looking at me with a teasing expression. He repeats himself.

'Well, I think this second roa was my turn. So it's your turn again.'

And though I know he is teasing, and I don't really have to do it, I'm happy to. Mr Henry is not a young man. And I love the chase!

It soon happens. I hear the bell. I hear the bark. I'm off again! Summoning all my energy and strength I charge towards the sounds, scramble up and down gullies, push through mud and lawyer vine, struggle up banks so steep they are more like cliffs. I'm terrified this bird might get away. I'm panting from effort, but anxiety makes me even more breathless. I'm huffing and heaving. I have injuries all over my body. I have to get there. I must prevent the bird escaping or the dog hurting it. My pulse is racing with anxiety as well as oxygen. I'm all nerves and urgency. Will I make it in time?

I do! Now discovering what Foxy has caught is almost as exciting as the chase: will it be a kākāpō or a kiwi? When the commotion starts to die down the next bit will be exciting, too, will it be old or young? Male or female? Hurt or in good condition?

It's a kākāpō. Mr Henry runs up and we examine it gently and carefully in case Foxy has hurt it but it seems okay. I feel very protective of kākāpō when they seem to trustingly accept what we're doing – it makes me care about saving them even more.

Two roa and one kākāpō equals a full cage so we head back to camp.

But don't think that is the end of the day's work: it's only half. Now we need to keep the birds fed and healthy until we release them – and that takes a lot of toil, too.

CHAPTER EIGHT

Date: July, 1895
Bird tally: roa x 40; kiwi x 27; kākāpō x 37
Injuries tally:
- *My knee hurts but it is inside it, a joint or bone or something, as the injury cannot be seen on my skin.*
- *I have seventeen infected sandfly bites, but I think I'm becoming used to them, because apart from them, there're not as many and they're not as irritating as when I first arrived.*

This is what's been happening:

The days pass quickly and I like the rhythm of our lives.

Whenever the weather looks settled we pack the boat, go to a part of Dusky Sound that we know has a good bird population, unpack and set up camp. Foxy leaps about sticking his nose into everything, sometimes getting in the way, but he is a cheerful sort of dog.

We go into the bush. We capture birds. When we have three birds in our backpack cage we bring them back to the camp and put them in the transporting cages, the original ones Mr Henry made, which have handles on each side. We cover the cages with scrim so the sandflies can't get in – if a bird can't get away, sandflies bite them almost to death. We put heavier sacking or branches over the scrim for kiwi and roa, to make it darker so they get less stressed. Even so, they often use their long beaks to poke holes in the scrim, and kākāpō will gnaw at the slats Mr *Carpenter* Henry used to form bars on the cages.

We go back into the bush and wait for Foxy to lead us to more birds, which we catch and put in the backpack cage. When it is full we take it back to camp. We may do this only once or we may do it several times before the day ends. Then we start our camp duties.

'We should call the camp a food and feeding station,' says Mr Henry to me as I start getting tucker – yesterday's fish, cooked – for Foxy. I'm now used to him only talking when he has something to say.

'That's true,' I say. 'First we feed the dog, then the birds, then ourselves.'

Mr Henry nods but he is looking at our captives. I may love the chase but Mr Henry loves the birds. He's talking to them while Foxy's looking worriedly at what I'm putting out for his dinner. Foxy's had to learn to eat fish but doesn't like it much.

'There now.' Mr *Fatherly* Henry is crooning to the birds, hoping to settle them. 'There now my old friends, there now, the cages are just for a night or two.' As he talks he puts his head on one side to gaze at them, looking a little like a bird himself. 'Soon you'll know freedom again.'

We both start searching for food they like.

Finding food for kākāpō isn't too hard.

'Their favourite food is rimu berries, and they love mapou, fuschia and panax berries,' Mr Henry told me when we caught the first ones.

Well, there were plenty of berries in the autumn but not so many now. However, since then we've discovered they'll eat just about anything that grows: fern roots, seeds, green shoots, fungi, stems, foliage.

'First night, so we won't have to get much,' I say hopefully. On the first night of captivity kākāpō are often sulky or sad, staring out of the cage and not eating. I feel sorry for them and can imagine how they must feel. I suppose Mr Henry is teaching me to think like that. But the second day they cheer up, perhaps because they are getting used to captivity or maybe they're getting pretty hungry, and they gobble up food. Some have even eaten bits of apple and carrot when berries are short and we can't find other food they like.

Roa and kiwi won't eat at all when put in a cage, first, second or any night, we discovered.

When we realised that, Mr Henry had a shrewd idea.

'What if one of us holds their legs, while the other open their beaks and drop in a few grubs?' he suggested.

'They might get the idea,' I said, wondering what I would do if someone held my arms and legs, opened my mouth and dropped food into it. His scheme was a complete success, however, and now we simply open their beaks and pop in the morsels on their first night. They quickly get the idea. By the second or third night we don't have to force them as they're eating without any fuss and wolf up whatever grubs and insects we drop into their cages.

Tonight it takes quite a while to find enough of the insects, worms and seeds they like. While I'm hunting I think I see a stoat, which is unusual, but to be expected, as we know they live in the bush on the mainland preying on the birds. I have seen rats, too.

After we've fed the birds we feed ourselves.

Usually I cook while Mr Henry writes up his notes.

Sometimes he plays his tin whistle, mostly popular songs from the goldfields. Tonight he is playing a sailors' sea shanty while I'm melting fat in the frying pan to cook bacon, which is always good, and preserved penguin eggs, which I'm getting used to. For afters we spread biscuits with tinned butter and tinned jam and drink tea.

If only Arthur could see me – catching insects and worms like a child and cooking like one of my sisters.

We have enough birds to fill the transporting cages – and the weather's not threatening so we break camp, stow the boat, and take the birds to Resolution Island. I love letting them go.

We beach *Pūtangi*, we lift out the cages, we open their doors. It takes a minute for the birds to realise the cage is open, then they tentatively put a foot or beak out, pause a moment, realise they are free, and scurry, scurry, scurry, like a mouse, to the nearest bit of cover. Helped by their colours, they disappear. They are simply gone. No sign, no movement, no noise, nothing.

The feeling of having done something completely good comes over both of us then. We have rescued them from the sneaky predators of the mainland. We know they hate being baled up by the dog, being captured and caged, being force-fed (well, the kiwi and roa must hate that), being transported on water – all land birds hate water – and then being put in a strange place. But we know what they don't know – that they are safe. There are no cunning ferrets, sly stoats, wily weasels, no ravaging rats on Resolution Island. From now on they can live and breed in peace.

We are not so anxious about the roa as there were already quite a few on Resolution Island, but we have decided to also release a few of each kind of bird on Anchor Island as a double surety.

After we release the birds we head back to our island home. It's easy to pull into our little cove, unload everything and then pull up the boat. We lug most things up to the house (I'm glad I made good steps), dropping one or two items into the storehouse on the way past, and have everything hanging to dry, or put away, before it's dark. Scrag and Yellow are pleased to see us – or simply hope we will have damper crusts for them – and Piopio comes cheerfully inside to check us over, so it's very welcoming. Then we have the warmth of a good fire and warm, dry beds.

I can tell you I'm really enjoying this strange and lonely life on Resolution Island.

Who wouldn't?

CHAPTER NINE

Date: October, 1895

Bird tally: roa x 81; kiwi x 39; kākāpō x 94

Injuries tally: ?

- *Shoulder should be painful, from boom hitting me in a williwaw, but it's not.*
- *Many sandfly bites but they are not infected and I have stopped counting them.*

This is what's been happening:

Father and Mr Henry agreed I would come to Dusky Sound for fifteen months – a calendar year plus a second winter – but I sent a letter to Mother and Father, via the *Hinemoa*, asking if I could stay longer and they agreed I could stay for one more year.

Father wrote back:

Mr Maitland informs me Mr Henry has sent glowing reports about you and said your aptitude and application is a credit to yourself and to your parents. I am pleased you wish to continue to apply yourself to this endeavour and you have my permission to continue in your present occupation.

Mother wrote, too:

I am very pleased you are held in high esteem but wish to remind you, Son, this is only an extension of your time in Fiordland. Eventually you will have to leave and begin carving out a career in society.

Nancy wrote:

Andrew, when you catch fish and birds you could examine the contents of their stomachs to see what they eat – that is the sort of research I'd like to do. Do you know that there are women attending Otago University and two have nearly finished medical degrees? I am planning to go to university so when you come home would you please help persuade Mother and Father it is a good idea?

Whew! How do you reply to that?

Victoria had different questions:

Did you like Mr Buller, the world-famous ornithologist, who visited? Could I come and visit, too, and take home a kākāpō parrot to live in a cage in the living room?

The twins wrote, each using one side of the same page of paper:

Have you been chased by Māori from the 'Lost Tribe'? We would love to catch birds and walk in the bush and sail on boats, too. You are very lucky.

I write back to all of them, and explain what I do to the twins:

The birds and bush are only part of my life. I garden and cook as well, especially now that we have nearly caught enough birds and they are thriving on their new island homes. We still catch a few, but mostly for aviaries, or we send skins and feathers to museums. We're sending some live roa to Dunedin because a man wants to breed them and make a business of selling them to people to rid their potato patches of wireworms.

As their big brother I also give the twins advice: *I certainly don't believe stories about a lost tribe of cannibal Māori hiding in the bush, and you shouldn't either.*

Sometimes when I'm in the bush and see soft, springy moss with little swirly patterns in it, I'm reminded of my sisters' flowery dresses – and then I think about how long it is since I've seen them.

There is no letter from Arthur. I wonder if he has new friends now and doesn't care about what I'm doing in this lonely place.

Arthur would be impressed if he came sailing with me today – and he'd be scared.

Let me explain: a map of Dusky Sound shows long ribbons of water fingering inland. They're marked as Vancouver and Wet Jacket Arms and most people would expect them to be sheltered from crosswinds and easy to sail or row in.

They are not.

That's mainly because of what Mr Henry calls

'williwaws', which are sudden, wild gusts of wind coming from anywhere – spinning out of mountain ridges, out of gullies, out of gaps in the cliffs – which leap about the sound, twisting and coiling round the boat from all directions, so it feels like we're no more than a leaf in a drain.

And we know what happens to leaves in drains.

Arthur does. Dunedin also gets plenty of rain.

Today a williwaw wind meets our sail and the boat leans so far over I'm scared it will capsize. Mr Henry and I move over, to put our weight on the opposite side to the lean. I wish *Pūtangi* had a bigger keel.

But it gets worse.

A williwaw hits the water in front of us, which makes the waves stand up. The boat bucks.

'Drop the sail. Grab it as it falls. Don't let it get swept over!' yells Mr Henry, who is holding the tiller with both hands, trying to keep control as the boat is buffeted this way and that.

I drop the sail and thrust it, all unfolded and higgledy piggledy under the seat. The boat rears and jumps about like a live animal that's been hit and before I can catch my breath some of the things on board which have been dislodged begin to fall about. I look every which way as I'm terrified water will enter the boat or some of our things will fall out but at the same time I'm working hard to pack things back where they should be. A bit of water spills in but there is so much gear on board neither of us can bail it out. Then, just as we have things pretty much put right, the wind changes direction again, comes from somewhere else and the problems start all over again.

I'd like Arthur to understand that even apart from williwaws, sailing here is scary because the weather can change very quickly. We can be sailing along and it's calm and we're thinking what a lovely day it is and what a lovely time we're having, when suddenly a southerly storm could come roaring in, straight from the Antarctic Ocean, and sweep absolutely everything in front of it – including a little boat called *Pūtangi* and a conservator called Henry with his apprentice conservator called Andrew. If this happened we'd be totally at the mercy of shrieking, gale-force winds; I've seen waves as high as the mast, which is terrifying. Add to that a southerly storm brings driving rain, which makes visibility minimal and penetrates our jackets, trousers and boots. Chilled right through, it is almost impossible to handle the boat.

To be honest, though we have seen these southerly storms, we have never actually been in one – Mr Henry makes very sure we do everything we can to avoid it. As soon as he sees storm clouds gathering on the horizon, we make for home if we can, otherwise to the nearest camp, and sit it out, for as many days as necessary.

No, Arthur has no idea of how dangerous it can be on the water – and I'd like him to know.

Our work here is a success.

We've caught and released lots of birds, mostly on Resolution Island, but also on Anchor Island. We have cut and formed tracks on both islands so we can keep an eye on them.

Because we spend less time catching birds we've been able to complete the house and it's every bit as good as those in Dunedin. It has an iron roof and we've wallpapered it and painted the door and around the windows. There's a bedroom each, which is good because I feel as if I have my own private place (not that I have anything private to keep or do in my private space!).

There's a fire and we burn green wood to create a smoky, blue haze which deters sandflies. Mr Henry said he would build shelves, a table and chairs, but he's even made easy chairs as well as the upright ones we use at the table. We have a scullery area for cooking and washing.

We stuff our boots with dried ferns and brush

to dry them and have a place to hang our oilskins and wet clothes to dry. There's no veranda because you can never sit outside here, the sandflies are too vicious.

We are going to build a boat shed with walls of punga and a shingled roof of split rimu. We've already put in tramway-like railings to slide *Pūtangi* from where-the-shed-will-be to the water, and Mr Henry designed a capstan so we can easily haul her back up on them.

Mr Henry has praised my path made of stones and crushed shells – and my very good steps – which starts at the boat ramp, winds past the storehouse, the vegetable garden and the site of our original canvas camp, to curve up to the house.

The vegetable garden is now really big, *Mr Never-Sit-and-Do-Nothing* Henry gets me to do almost all the work in the garden. Mr Henry has not been very successful at enticing paradise ducks to stay on the cleared ground but Scrag and Yellow, always hoping for a scrap from the kitchen or worm from the garden, and Piopio, always curious about anything different, keep us company when we work around the house and garden. So do Skite and Mine. Skite and Mine are two kākā Mr Henry stole from their nest. One ordinary day I was breaking up soil in the vegetable garden when there was the most enormous commotion. I looked up and saw Mr Henry bumbling up the track. He was hunched over and every kākā in the area was screaming and diving at him.

'Mr Henry! Sir! What's the matter?'

I was worried and ran towards him. Had he cut himself? Had a heart attack? Why was he hunched over like that, with his arms wrapped round his body?

'All-all-all right,' he huffed as he came up to me. The adult kākā continued to shriek and scream. 'I'm all right Andy lad, all right. The parents and other birds are just ganging up on me.'

Kākā
(parrot)

Very noisy. Their call is usually loud and grating but can be melodious, or be just a straight note.

Nest, feed and live in forest trees and often move in flocks. They eat insects (especially wood-boring ones like huhu), and the seeds, flowers and fruits of some native beech and podocarp.

weighing from 14 to 20 oz

grey-white crown

red tinge to neck feathers

18 inches

orange and scarlet flashes under the wing

brown/green/grey plumage

crimson under the body

dark grey to black beak

yellow tinge to the cheek

strongly patterned brown/green/grey plumage

And they were. They flew from low-hanging branch to low-hanging branch, they whizzed past us, they circled above us, they screeched loudly and non-stop.

'What's happening? Why are they doing that? What's wrong with you?' I felt panicky.

'Come. Come quickly,' was all he said as he stumbled and rushed towards the house. I followed him – and the protesting, diving, shrieking birds followed us both.

'Look!' he said, once we were inside and the door closed. He opened his jacket front and placed two very young kākā on the table. They jostled each other. Foxy put his nose up to the table edge nearest them.

'Mr Henry – you – I – you – *stole* them!' I must have looked shocked because Mr Henry sounded a bit apologetic when he answered.

'These are parrots, Andy lad,' he said. 'Honey-eating *parrots*.'

I realised what he meant: we could train them as

you can train a parrot – and that is what we've done, using food as encouragement. They now come immediately he calls their names, or when he plays *Yankee Doodle* on his whistle. They are good company and sometimes we even take them with us on our bird hunts. They don't like being in the cages while we're sailing there but once we set up camp they enjoy tent life – I think because they use every opportunity to steal from our provisions! They will do anything to attract notice and when we give them attention, they strut about and look at the other as if to say: *I'm the favourite! See! See!*

We are proud to be known as rescuers and caretakers of endangered birds.

We're very comfortable, we enjoy our pets, fishing, garden vegetables.

I'm allowed to stay on in Dusky Sound for a bit longer.

Foxy continues to work energetically.

Mr Henry thinks well of me.

One day people will talk about *Andrew Burt, Kākāpō and Kiwi Keeper.*

Everything is perfect.

CHAPTER TEN

Date: March, 1896

Bird tally: roa x 164; kiwi x 53; kākāpō x 171

Injuries tally:

• A few cuts on my hands from fishing.

• A few scratches on my face from lawyer vine.

• A few sandfly bites here and there.

• Nothing very bad.

This is what's been happening:

The *Cavalier* is here.

Mr Henry, Foxy and I have just checked birds on Parrot Island when suddenly a schooner with a group of tourists on board appears. They have come to meet Mr Henry, so while he and Captain Roderique exchange greetings, all the other passengers are listening with wide-open eyes. A few have wide-open mouths.

'You're a lucky young man to be in the company of such an eminent New Zealander,' one of them says to me.

'He calls the birds "the oldest New Zealanders",' I reply, and that seems to amuse them, as they smile. I look at him through their eyes and see a slight man with a pleasant expression, speaking in a gently hesitant voice. A nice man but not a person to get excited about, you'd think.

However, it seems the whole country is talking about Mr Henry's work and he's a sort of hero – they came hoping to see 'the famous Mr Henry'. That made Mr Henry shy and mumbly – until he realised some of the people treating him with respect were from Otago University and the newspaper. Now he's no longer self-conscious and says they're a cracker of a group.

There's a boy on board, too, Charlie Johnstone. He's from Cromwell and travelling with his parents. I think of Arthur and wish he could come as a tourist on the *Cavalier*. Charlie Johnstone stares at me with pale-blue eyes.

'You a real bushman, or can you read?' he asks. Except he isn't really asking, he's challenging me. Whatever I answer I'll be either a skite or illiterate.

'I'm a follower of the theories of Mr Charles Darwin, and doing ornithological fieldwork in the bush,' I say, hoping big words will confuse him. The long winter evenings made me bored enough to read Mr Henry's books.

'What's ornithological mean?' He stands too close and is a bit taller than I am.

'Bird studies.'

'This'll be handy, then,' he says, pulling a shanghai out of his pocket and pretending to fire it at a shag flying past.

'Maybe.'

'I've got a good eye for hitting a target.'

A good eye? His eyes are cold, not good. I start to say 'we're here to save birds, not kill them' but change the subject instead. 'Bet you didn't know there're tree stumps here that Captain Cook's men cut down? They're across there, if you go round those rocks and then between the islands to Astronomer's Point.'

'Just because you know things about this place doesn't mean you know more than me about other things.' He shoves his shanghai roughly back into his pocket.

Not a great beginning. Arthur would have been interested in Captain Cook. But maybe Charlie has been the only boy on the *Cavalier* and isn't pleased the other passengers are now giving me some of the attention he's used to getting. Or maybe he's jealous of me because he'd like to have a real job away from home instead of living with his parents and going on holiday with them.

While Charlie and I are talking, it's decided Mr Henry will board the *Cavalier* to guide it to Pickersgill Harbour and I, with one or two others, will follow in

Pūtangi. Then, because Mr *Mistaken* Henry has seen Charlie and me talking, he thinks we have struck up a friendship and he suggests Charlie be the one to go with me in our little dinghy. Straight away Charlie shows himself to be a more natural sailor than I'll ever be, but at least it isn't rough so he doesn't see me being scared. I hope he notices I'm more practised at rowing than he is.

It should be good to have a friend to talk to, but everything seems to be a competition with Charlie Johnstone.

That first day we go to Pickersgill, show the sightseers where Captain Cook's *Resolution* was moored, show them the tree stumps at Astronomer's Point and then end up showing them the way back to Facile Harbour. The tourists listen carefully to Mr Henry's every word. I tell Charlie about the first-ever European ship being built there, and the first-ever European shipwreck being there, which all happened in the 1790s when sealers started coming to New Zealand. I show him a punga path, maybe a hundred years old, made of the trunks laid side by side, probably made by them. I describe what it's like to chase a ringing bell on a dog that's found a kākāpō. He hardly listens.

Today we're fishing on the *Pūtangi* and I explain how anyone can catch fish in Dusky Sound, they practically jump onto the hook, but when Charlie drops a line he brings up an octopus. He doesn't actually hook it – it hangs onto the sinker of the line and Charlie tries to knock it off with an oar, which is difficult because as soon as he gets one arm off another one will have twined around.

Neither of us is willing to actually grab it with our hands to dislodge it. It finally decides it doesn't want to be on the line and drops off – and Charlie doesn't want to do any more fishing.

'There could be seals here,' I tell him. 'I haven't seen one, but once we saw what must have been the

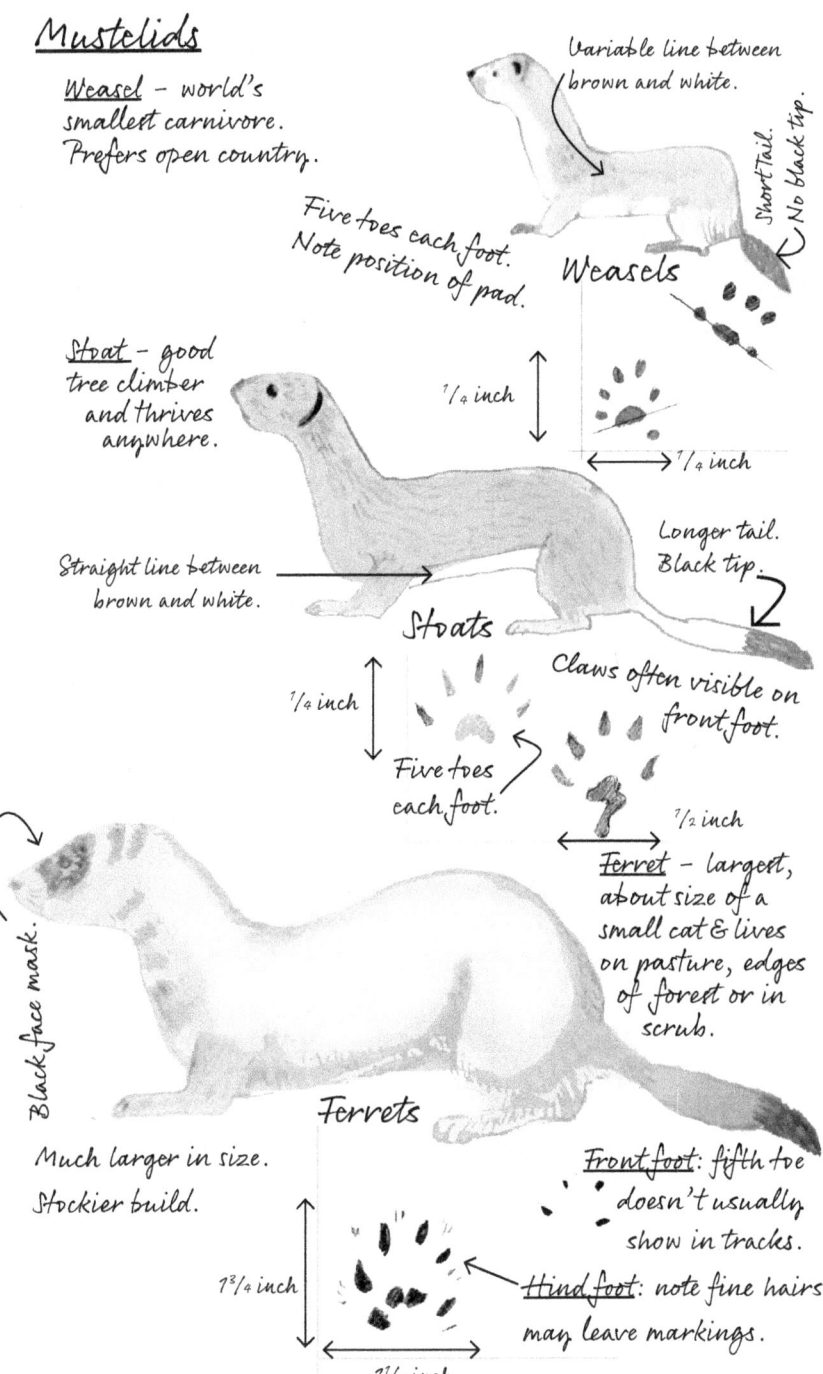

wake of one when it dived. We didn't see it come up anywhere, though. It knew how to hide.'

'You think you're special because you've been rescuing some stupid birds,' says Charlie. 'You don't own this place, you know.'

'I'm not saying I do, but Mr Henry wants to make, not just Resolution Island, this whole fiord a sanctuary. Make it safe for seals, and every sort of bird, as well as the ones that can't fly. If we can stop the hunting, the seals might come back to Dusky Sound. Mr Henry's seen a live seal. On land they look like round black rocks and unless they move –'

'Oh, shut up for a while.' Charlie looks around. I don't think he's looking for seals. Perhaps I am saying too much, but it's such a novelty to have someone my age to talk to.

'Hey! What's that?' Charlie points across at a sort of cove within Facile Harbour.

'What?' I look in the direction he is pointing. I think I see something small, grey-brown above and pale underneath, run, well move, actually *ripple* might be a better word, across gravel and small stones beside a large boulder. If I do see something move, it is instantly gone behind the rock.

'I can't see anything,' I say.

'It's a weasel. It's chasing a weka.'

'Don't be stupid, that's Resolution Island, that's where birds are safe from weasels.'

'It is. It definitely is. I know a weasel when I see one. It's chasing a weka.'

I'd think Charlie was just teasing me except that I think - but only *think* - I saw that movement. I don't answer him but pull hard on the right oar to make the boat swing in the direction of the cove and then start rowing as hard as I possibly can.

'Well people won't think you're so clever now, will they, you and Mr Henry. You've been catching birds and putting them on an island that has weasels on it. Wait till everyone hears about that.'

My heart is pounding, but not from rowing, as

I pull as hard as I can on the oars. If it really is a weasel – *pull back* – then all our captured birds are at risk – *oars forward*. If it really is a weasel – *pull back* – then all our work has been in vain – *oars forward*. If it really is a weasel – *pull back* – we may as well pack up and leave – *oars forward* – on the *Cavalier* today – *pull back* –

I don't even try to explain to Charlie that what he's saying could ruin my whole life; worse, it could ruin Mr Henry's whole life; worst of all, it could take the lives of all our birds. All of them. It can't be true.

I beach *Pūtangi* near the large boulder, hurl the grapnel high above the high-water mark and rush everywhere. Everywhere. Charlie realises I'm panicking, or perhaps he wants to prove he's right, and for a while he searches, too, though half-heartedly. We look in all directions, along the beach, behind the boulder, by rough vegetation, under a bank. We search for what I call 'evidence' and Charlie calls 'proof'. He gets bored then, and tries to hit a shag, perched nearby with its wings held out to dry, with his shanghai. Next he aims it at two gulls which fly off. He sits on the big boulder for a while.

There are no tracks, no sign of feathers, nothing. There is brittle seaweed, dried into delicate traceries like preserved ferns, and real ferns emerging softly from the edge of the bush. There is a flax bush and its flowers – kōradi – edging open, then curling back to release their seeds, little black eyes that scatter out to seek moist, dark places. I shudder.

Charlie insists we leave.

I have to agree. I'd like to keep looking but there's no point as there is absolutely nothing to see. It is a deserted beach. There are no birds. There is no weasel. There are no tracks. There is no point in staying.

There are stones and bits of broken shell and twigs and leaves and low brush and fresh seaweed and dried seaweed.

Nothing else.

Back on board the *Cavalier* Charlie rushes breathlessly to be first to tell Mr Henry about seeing the weasel. I hold back: this is not exciting news, if it turns out to be true it is devastating information.

'A weasel, now, a weasel, you saw? Maybe you saw one of Mr Haast's great big eagles at the same time, did you, lads?' Mr Henry laughs at what Charlie's saying. He has been enjoying having company and thinks this story is part of the fun.

'I live in Cromwell, Mr Henry. I've seen a weasel chasing rabbits many times,' says Charlie. I notice he speaks respectfully to an adult but I can tell he doesn't like Mr Henry not taking him seriously.

'Or did you see a couple of moa, Charlie?' He keeps thinking Charlie is playing a trick on him, but then he looks at me. He knows I would never joke about anything so serious, or perhaps he sees the miserable look on my face. He stops laughing.

'Is he serious, Andy lad? You were there?'

'Charlie is serious,' I say.

Mr Henry's face goes blank. There is no colour in it, no expression in it. He motions to me to step away from everyone else. He wants to talk privately. He pauses before he speaks, looking at me gravely.

'Did Charlie really see a weasel? Would he recognise one if he saw it?' His voice is almost hoarse as he tries to keep it pitched low. 'Did you see one? Did you see anything? Yes? No? What did you see?'

I tell him exactly what happened, that we'd been fishing and bickering a bit and then Charlie suddenly pointed to something and I looked and though I couldn't say I had seen any 'thing' I did think I had seen low, slithering movement on the stones where he was pointing. Mr Henry nods and nods.

'Go on, go on, what else? What else?'

I wish I could be more definite but I can't.

The *Cavalier* will depart this afternoon, but all the fun and novelty of having company has already left. Has Charlie really seen a weasel on our island sanctuary? As he boards to leave he gives me an understanding look. I think he now realises how bad this is.

CHAPTER ELEVEN

Date: March–April, 1896

Bird tally: no change, we are no longer catching and releasing.

Injuries tally: None. Unless a sense of doom is an injury.

This is what's been happening:

    The *Cavalier* isn't even quarter-way to Five Fingers when Mr Henry stows a billhook, spade and axe in the hull and unwinds the capstan to release *Pūtangi*. The oars are in place so I rush to unlash the mast, which Mr Henry, when he gets on board, manoeuvres upright. He runs up the sail and is securing the clew to the boom while I shove at the stern. As soon as she begins to slide into the water Foxy, who knows what to do, and I leap in. Though Mr Henry has moved quickly, it is in his usual, precise, careful way. The same way he speaks to Foxy.

'Your best work now, boy. This has to be your best work.' He places the muzzle over Foxy's mouth. Mr Henry knows Foxy won't even try to hunt unless the muzzle is on. He buckles it in place and gives the dog a searching look, as if to see if he can understand his words. Foxy flicks his tail twice and his brown eyes gaze serenely, unblinkingly, back. I can tell he's looking forward to whatever Mr Henry has in store for him – but probably doesn't know what he means.

Scrag and Yellow remain on our beach, tossing and foraging at seaweed as we leave. There isn't much wind so the sail doesn't make much difference and I row without speaking. The plaintive cry of a black-backed gull keens across the water, ribbons of amber kelp stream from a partly submerged rock. I look back at that rather than look at Mr Henry; I don't like the frantic expression on his face and the agitated look in his eyes.

'It's probably not true,' I say, after a while. 'That Charlie might be wanting attention. He might think people will take notice of what he said and that'll make him as important as me – I mean us.'

Mr Henry looks at me as if I'm speaking Chinese. Foxy looks at me as if I'm speaking Chinese.

'Charlie thought I was skiting. He might have said he saw it to make me shut up,' I explain.

'Ah.' Mr Henry looks at me thoughtfully. 'Jealousy, you mean?'

'Yes. Just boys fighting ... you know ...'

Mr Henry shakes his head, then shakes it again. You'd think he was trying to shake something insignificant but mildly annoying, like slaters, out of his hair. Foxy flops his head on one side, in imitation – or sympathy.

'You could well be right, Andrew,' he says as he eases the sail a little to try and get wind. 'I know what jealousy can make people do.'

Father told me people criticised scientific studies Mr Henry sent from Te Anau to the *Otago Witness*, arguing he could not be taken seriously as he was not a trained ornithologist. The sail catches a bit of wind and fills a little, which makes rowing slightly easier but there's not enough wind to really move the boat. After a while he speaks again.

'Howsoever, it may be true. And we must find out. Find out? Find it. No matter what.'

I row till we get to the fishing spot where we saw – where Charlie *said* he saw and I *thought* I saw – the weasel, and point across at the little bit of stony beach in Facile Harbour. 'Over there, in front, and then to the side of the big boulder.'

'It moved in front of the boulder and then to the side?'

'I thought I saw *movement* in front of it and then *movement* to the side, which disappeared ...' I consider my words. 'Or *stopped*. I'll row over there now?'

Mr Henry nods grimly. I pull hard on the oars and am soon beaching *Pūtangi* on the stony shore. Straight away Mr Henry steps onto the hard mix of small stones, broken shells and grit. Foxy jumps out.

'Wayo, Foxy,' he says immediately, then looks at me. 'An element of surprise gives him the best chance of finding something.' While he speaks he must be assessing the shore and, realising there is no sand on which to see tracks, goes immediately to the boulder, looks at the front and then steps round behind it. There is nothing, of course: more small stones, bits of dried, brownish seaweed, and twigs.

'Could have been a rat, scavenging,' says Mr Henry when I join him after securing *Pūtangi*. He is being hopeful. A rat wouldn't be as bad as a weasel. There is light brush – penguin grass and coprosma – on the small bank between the boulder on the shoreline and the edge of the bush. He roughly clears it away with the billhook, telling me to use the spade to dig at the overhanging bank and see if there is a hole. I do. There isn't. I stop digging where the bank stops. Behind that is a clump of flax, which is at the base of a sheer cliff face.

'Well, whatever the creature was, it's gone and left no trace.' Mr Henry's voice is without emotion, unlike his eyes, which – how can I describe it – which are *glaring* at the cliff.

Foxy comes trotting happily back. He could have been with the twins and returning from a pleasant Sunday stroll along Glen Road, for all the interest he shows in the surrounding bush and beach.

'So there's nothing more we can do?'

'If we can't track it, we'll trap it.'

This morning Mr Henry tells me to catch fish while he's building boxes.

'Keep anything you hook. It's not for us to eat, so it doesn't matter if it's red cod, spotties, just whatever you catch.'

While I'm fishing he finishes the boxes and then bores large holes in their sides.

'We'll put rat traps inside them,' he says grimly, his mouth in a thin, straight line. 'If there is a weasel anywhere on Resolution Island, these will kill it.' This is a different Mr Henry from the one who talks to birds.

We load boxes, traps and fish onto *Pūtangi*. There is no rush today and we go at the speed I call Mr *Non-Haste* Henry, working at a deliberate and steady pace, ignoring all obstacles.

'Even if a weka is attracted to the smell of fish, it won't be able to get into the box,' he explains. 'But weasels are curious creatures and if one comes sneaking about, it will smell the fish and find a hole to enter. After that I have great faith the trap will do its job.'

There is no wind so we don't bother putting up the mast. I push off, then fit the oars into the rowlocks and begin rowing. I'm good at this now and look forward to showing Father what a smooth rhythm I've developed. There are so many things I've learned since I've been here. I think Father – and Mother and the girls – will regard me in a new way when they see me.

After a while Mr Henry fits Foxy's muzzle. 'Today,

boy, today. Do your very best,' he commands, briefly holding his hand on top of the dog's head. 'See if you can find a weasel today while we set these traps.' There seems to be a note of pleading in his voice.

Foxy does not find a weasel.

We come back the next day, and the day after. A weasel doesn't like decaying matter, let alone stinking fish, so we replace the untouched fish while making sure the traps are still set. It takes a while to wash the stinky fish smell from my hands and the seawater is cold.

The traps don't catch anything.

Today we're putting poison in the boxes in case the weasel did come but was suspicious of the appearance of traps. We load up *Pūtangi,* we take the muzzle off Foxy, we go to what we've named Boulder Beach. We open the boxes to remove the traps and the putrid fish. We take the boxes to new positions and place fresh fish inside, which Mr Henry sprinkles with strychnine.

'Careful now, Andy lad,' says Mr Henry. 'It doesn't

look much different from sugar, but even a small amount can kill you.'

We toss branches about the boxes so they look more naturally part of the landscape. We call Foxy, who hasn't found anything, and leave.

Today we check the poisoned fish. The lids are on the boxes. The poisoned fish is in the boxes. There are no dead weasels. Foxy vaguely sniffs around the edge of the bush but doesn't find anything to entice him further away. Everything looks exactly as we left it.

'Nothing. Nothing. Not even a rat,' says Mr Henry, who has always been a quiet man but these days is silent almost all the time. When he does speak, he mutters and I think he is really talking to himself, not to me. I wish I could answer – talk to him the way Mother used to talk to me – and tell him I really do understand how terrible Charlie's words were. I can't. But they were murdering words.

Murdering birds.

This evening we're sitting looking at the fire when unexpectedly Mr Henry speaks. He tells me he feels partly responsible for the birds being killed.

'If only I'd known then what I know now,' he says. 'When I lived at Te Anau I used to ferry people up and down the lake. They loved to see all the birds – not just kiwi and kākāpō but the different sorts of ducks and pigeons, songbirds. Beautiful.' He shuts his eyes for a moment, remembering. 'But one day some fellows hired me to take them down the lake so they could let loose a batch of ferrets near the Lake Manapouri end. Ferrets! A whole batch of them!'

Mr Henry had been with men who released ferrets! How could he do that!

'If I'd only known then what I know now,' he repeats, as if reading my thoughts. 'At the time farmers were giving up farming because rabbits were eating all the grass they had planted for sheep and they couldn't make any money.'

I keep looking at the fire but peep at him out of the corner of my eye. He looks weary and sad.

'It seemed simple. We knew ferrets are wily, sneaky killers and we thought they would quickly get rid of the rabbits. But that's the trouble: they are wily, sneaky killers, but killers of everything, not just rabbits. They kill birds – all birds, any birds – without discrimination. Of course it's not just ferrets, other people released weasels and stoats and they are just as bad.' He frowns and his eyes grow hooded as he broods on the habits of those three animals.

'But ferrets are the worst of all creatures! I hate them. They move like shadows, eye up their prey, then slither in for the kill ... almost snake-like.' He almost hisses the 's' in 'slither', 'almost' and 'snake'.

'The very next morning we saw one of those ferrets four miles from where we had released them. That's how quickly they travel.' He is shaking his head. 'And Andy, would you believe, three years after that there wasn't a single one of those birds, not a kākāpō, a kiwi, a weka, or their tracks, to be seen along the shores of Lake Manapouri. But there were ferret tracks everywhere. They didn't hang about on the lake shore, either: inland, in the gullies and streams of the forested hills behind the lake, the teals and grey ducks completely vanished. Tragic.' He turns towards me and sighs as he adds. 'And I had a hand in it, Andrew. I'm partly responsible.'

'Mr Henry, if they hadn't got you to take them they would have paid someone else.' I feel sorry for him and his distress.

'Maybe,' he says. 'Maybe. But *maybe* I should have realised what would happen and refused.'

There is nothing I can say to that.

This morning Mr Henry caught a weka using a wire loop on the end of a stick, then wrung its neck. Now I'm dragging it around the beach so the weasel can smell its bloody traces on the gravel. Mr Henry calls to me that I'm to haul it in and out of the nearby bush, too, hoping the general scent of blood will attract the weasel.

Foxy watches in disbelief.

Mr Henry carefully sprinkles strychnine on the weka. I can feel he wants to stay in case the weasel appears, but knows it is more likely to come out if he isn't here. He must trust his schemes to do their work.

'If only we had rabbit carcasses,' he says. 'Weasels love rabbit.'

As we row away he almost quivers with anxiety, like Foxy, after he has scented prey.

Again, nothing.

I would not have believed Mr Henry capable of today's plan.

He has caught a weka parent with two chicks and, not muzzling Foxy this time, we are rowing over to tether it on Boulder Beach. The babies will be left to run free and cheep as they run around. The parent

(I think it is a father weka) will be anxious and keep calling them back very loudly and attract a weasel. It's not as good as actually killing the weasel but if one of the young ones is killed, we may at least have proof there is one there. If no chicks are killed then we can be pretty sure there is no weasel on the island. Foxy, sitting in the bow with his tail tucked as neatly as a cat's, knowing he may not hunt unless he is muzzled, doesn't take his eyes off the weka family.

I imagine describing this cruelty to my sisters and trying to explain it is because Mr Henry is resolute. I think Mother would understand, based on what she wrote in her most recent letter – before we even knew about the possibility of a weasel.

Always remember, she wrote, *that though there may be times Mr Henry seems a little too pedantic and careful, I dare to say it, even a little dull at times, this is his Life's Work. Accept his meticulousness, Andrew. You have all your life before you and will do many wonderful, marvellous things, I am sure.*

Mr Henry, however, is old and this may be the last important thing he does. Indeed, you may not fully understand how important it is to him until you are an old man yourself.

Mr Henry's Life's Work might be ruined by a small, sneaking bit of vermin. The death of a weka chick or the distress of its parent can't be measured against that, I'd tell the girls. And who knows? Perhaps, one day, as a result of what Mr Henry has taught me, they may see me do wonderful, marvellous things, as Mother suggested.

We're releasing the tethered weka. Both its babies are happy, healthy – and here. As a result of all the things we have done we can safely say there is no evidence of a weasel on Resolution Island. The birds we saved are still safe. I'll be able to write to Mother that Mr Henry's Life's Work is not in jeopardy and Mr Henry will write in his notes for Mr Maitland there is *no evidence*. But still he talks about the weasel with a quiet, lethal, scheming loathing. Perhaps he is not completely convinced.

Mr Henry is whistling.

Mr Henry: *whistling*.

I stayed at the homestead today because he said I should catch fish for our dinner and then dig more disgusting guano into the earth where we hope to grow currants. He and Foxy went up to do a bird count on Resolution Island and now they are home and whistling – well Foxy's wagging his tail in time to Mr Henry's whistling. I can't believe it.

'I climbed the track up Mt Phillips,' he says, 'to do a count of that area, and would you believe it, Andy lad? First thing I see is a young kākāpō – with its mother and in a lovely condition. Just a cracker of a bird.'

That is good news, but good enough to make him whistle?

'When the ferrets were released beside Lake

Manapouri,' he tells me, 'the kākāpō in the area were gone within months. It would be the same here. If a weasel were living on Resolution, there would hardly be a kākāpō left alive. And most certainly not a kākāpō chick.'

So tonight I'm using potatoes we've grown to make fishcakes with the moki I caught. We'll open a tin of jam and a tin of cream and have them with a queen pudding made from penguin eggs. There'll be enough for Foxy as it's a celebratory meal: there is not a weasel to be found.

Resolution Island is still a sanctuary for our birds.

CHAPTER TWELVE

Date: August, 1896

Bird tally: None really, though we'll be collecting a few to go to some aviaries and collectors.

Injuries tally: None really.

· A bit of a scratch on my chin, from pruning a gooseberry bush.

This is what's been happening:

'We have so many friends here, Andy lad, you may have to hold a farewell party,' Mr Henry says, putting down the tin whistle he's been playing. He often makes jokes these days. I suppose it's because he doesn't have to work so hard.

We're sitting by the boat shed on seats Mr Henry made out of planks. For a wonderful change there are hardly any sandflies – or perhaps I'm so used to them now I hardly notice their constant biting. It is quiet. The water in front of us is sleek and soft, each wave no more than a gentle wrinkling of satin fabric. Everything – the water, the bush, the sky, the air – feels soft and easy.

Scrag and Yellow run here and there, in front of us.

'Yes, you may get food soon,' Mr Henry says to them. 'Though you haven't done much to deserve it, you impudent rascals.'

They've been hovering around, hoping for leftovers as usual. Weka are always busy, either searching for food – or demanding it from us. They think we live here just to throw them scraps of stale sultana scone. I'm glad Mr Henry got these two to replace the ones Lassie killed all that long time ago.

'Good idea,' I say. 'Let's invite them all to a party.' I want to keep up his joke and stop myself from feeling sad about returning to Dunedin next month. Well, sad to leave, yes, but satisfied, too, because we know our work is finished. We've shifted nearly five hundred birds to Resolution and Anchor Islands, plus a few to Long Island, and they're doing well.

We have done what we set out to do. We have saved the kākāpō, roa and kiwi. Not only that, last autumn there was a lot of booming so we expect plenty of young ones to hatch this year, which means they will continue to multiply and thrive on their islands.

'Oh my darling, oh my darling, oh my darling Clementine,' Mr Henry's stiff fingers play two lines of *Clementine*, which the twins were learning to play when I left Dunedin. It has a lamenting tone, making me feel sad again. But I'm also, to be honest, a wee bit excited. I have plans for when I return to Dunedin and am looking forward to telling them to Arthur, as well as telling him about what we've done.

'You are lost and gone forever, oh my darling Clementine.' Two more lines from his whistle.

'You are saved, to live forever, oh my darling kākāpō,' is what I hear in my head. I wish I could show Father, Mother and the girls our birds. In fact, I wish the whole world could see how entertaining the

kākāpō are – the way they peer at us and then strut off as if to say, *'Well yes, I've met you but you're not particularly interesting and I have pressing duties to attend to.'* I'd like everyone to meet all the birds we've befriended. *Befriended* – I see what Mr Henry means.

'It's good you'll have these friends when I'm gone,' I say to Mr Henry, who whistles *'Yankee Doodle went to town, riding on a pony',* and is immediately answered by the long cool cries of Skite and Mine. They will fly back and be beside us in no time.

'Mine! Skite!' calls Mr Henry and whistles *'put a feather in his cap and called it macaroni.'* Sure enough, the two kākā sweep in to land nearby. They keep an eye on us while snapping sharp comments to one another – 'gossiping' Mr Henry calls it.

'You must wait and listen to the concert, you scallywags,' he says to them, smiling. 'It won't hurt you to listen to me for a bit. I'm always putting myself out for you.'

I love seeing Mr Henry so happy – especially compared to those days after Charlie said he saw a weasel. He may miss me a little when I leave but he has told me Dusky Sound is where he is the happiest he has been in his whole life. He repeats a couple of lines from *Clementine*. Skite and Mine consult each other, agree not to join in, then, in unison, stomp over to the railing by the boatshed and squat on it, frowning at us. When we don't do anything, they simultaneously swing over and hang upside down, watching to see our reaction. I click my fingers and hold out two sultanas. They swish to me, take them from my hand, then fly back to the railing.

I like thinking they'll go with Mr Henry and be company when he sets up a camp, or when he checks the released birds, even though they'll raid his food stores for sure. They'll be an audience for him to play to, too, as they often make noises back to his whistle – he says they are commenting on his skill.

The weka have seen the kākā eat the sultanas and stalk closer, hoping for treats.

'Hello friend.' I greet Piopio, who is swooping down to check on us while the kākā take up their discussion again. Piopio, too, will be company for Mr Henry – whenever we have a cup of tea he appears and takes small sips from it. Actually, he likes almost everything he finds on the table – oatmeal porridge, milk, biscuits. He plays hide and seek with his reflection in the mirror and sings sweet little melodies, sometimes while he's hopping about Mr Henry's head and shoulders. Great entertainment for him.

I'm pleased Mr Henry will have Skite and Mine, little Piopio, Scrag and Yellow and their chicks to keep him company when I'm gone. And Foxy of course.

A southern right whale suddenly blows close by. It must have been swimming around about all the time.

'Don't you be frightening our friends, Sir Whale,' calls out Mr Henry, and he begins playing an old sailors' shanty my father taught me. Sailors use tin whistles like Mr Henry's and it sounds really catchy so I grab a kōradi head, and rattle it while doing a couple of little jiggy, hornpipe steps to make us laugh.

A pair of paradise ducks arrive. Now it really is a party.

Then Mr Henry asks me about my plans for my future.

'I want to become a ranger for the Acclimatisation Society,' I say. 'I want to save all birds. There are the songbirds, they need help, too, just as much as the ground birds here.' I have found my Life's Work. I don't care whether or not I'm ever famous.

Mr Henry nods approvingly and looks pleased. The whale doesn't stay. The water is calm. The birds go about their business.

I leave on the *Hinemoa* next month.

And I helped Mr Henry save the birds.

CHAPTER THIRTEEN

Date: September, 1896
Bird tally: 2 pairs each roa, kiwi, kākāpō and various song birds, for transporting.
Injury tally: 0

This is what's been happening:

'When you are back in Dunedin, Andy lad, if anyone asks, I now regard myself as full-time caretaker-of-endangered-but-saved-ground-dwelling birds,' says Mr Henry.

We're on *Pūtangi* and spending my last days checking the birds on the islands and assessing their numbers in other parts of the Sound. We are also supposed to be collecting some specimens. The *Hinemoa* is due to collect me in two weeks.

It's like a farewell tour for me.

'We have to get these specimens because the

governor ordered them,' says Mr Henry. 'But after this I will try to completely avoid collecting birds as specimens for museums or collectors. What's more, I will catch them for relocation only if I am convinced they will be well looked after on their journey and on arrival at their zoo or aviary or whatever it is. From now on I will describe myself as caretaker, employed to protect them. Indeed, I am here to preserve all species, not reduce them.' Mr Henry sounds as if he were making a speech to a crowd.

As usual Foxy is sitting up in the prow, keeping an eye out for pirates I suppose, and I'm pulling on the oars. It is warmish but drizzling lightly, making distances deceptive and the light mysterious.

We have left Pigeon Island, passed Whidbey Point and the entrance to Cormorant Cove, and are heading into Goose Cove to check bird numbers, particularly roa numbers.

'Any wild bird becomes distressed – even dies – if kept too long in captivity,' he says. I know that.

I know that's why he prepared a little paddock for roa, and made a dark house of bungies so they can hide and avoid sandflies. Songbirds are difficult to keep caged. I sometimes wonder if they get so droopy because their singing hearts are broken.

'We will not start capturing them till three or four days before the *Hinemoa* is due. It is good you will be on board the boat to ensure their welfare as they travel,' he continues.

Resolution Island is alongside us, with Five Fingers Peninsula stretching to port and I glance at it as I imagine the voyage back to Dunedin. I was seasick on the trip here and didn't know what I was coming to. This time it'll be different: I'll be looking after our birds and at the end of the trip I'll see Mother and Father and the girls. I can imagine Arthur's face when I tell him my plans.

'Aarrrrhhhh,' Mr Henry makes the strangest noise. He half stands up in the boat.

We *never* stand up in the boat.

I look at him.

His face looks as if someone has plunged a huge corkscrew into his stomach and is turning it around. His face is *agonised*.

'No. No. No,' he hisses.

The corkscrew continues turning.

Now he points at the shore.

I, too, look across at the nearby beach.

We stare. We stare and stare.

There is a small, pale shape slinking over the sandy shore

We squint, trying to see better.

It is. It is.

It can't be.

It is.

Determined to keep it in sight, I dip the right oar into the water and pull hard. The boat veers towards the shore and I continue to slip the oars quietly through the water, not splashing, trying not to alert the moving, light-coloured form of our presence.

Because I'm rowing, I have my back to it but when I look over my shoulder it is casually moving about. Mr Henry doesn't take his eyes off it. I beach the boat, trying to prevent the rattle of oars in the rowlocks and look at it again. Perhaps the animal sees us or smells us, for it leaves the sand and slips – glides – around a jumble of dark, wet-looking stones to disappear under a mossy overhang.

It is. I've never seen one but I'm sure it is.

I know it is.

Mr Henry leaps from the boat and runs towards the stones. Foxy follows him.

I pull *Pūtangi* up and over the furrowed, pitted bedrock, then join him.

The tracks are distinct and swerve this way and that. There is a deeper print to the left – it has lunged there – lunged to seize something? Or because it heard something, saw something, smelt something? Us? The tracks end beside the stones, which are in front of the moss and root-festooned cavity.

Mr Henry squats and tries to peer into it. Seawater shushes close by, trees lean away from the water and rocks, flax and astelia grip the sheer bank to his left. Lushness everywhere. He can't see anything. I can't hear anything. What is it – weasel, ferret, stoat? Mr Henry reads my mind.

'It seems too big for a weasel – a bit bigger than a rat – almost big enough to be a stoat – must be a young stoat.' He is muttering and talking in a half-strangled voice as his eyes dart everywhere. His thoughts spill out.

'If it's a young stoat – that means the parents are – no – it can't be – no – that means the parents must be nesting and raising their young on Resolution – and may have been for the last six months – since that Charlie claimed –' While he speaks Mr Henry looks wildly along the beach, up to the trees, into the undergrowth, at our boat, then back at the pile of shiny, wet rocks in front of the mossy overhang.

'*Wayo* boy, *wayo*,' he commands. Foxy looks at him,

confused at being given an order when his muzzle's off. He shows no interest, senses nothing unusual. He doesn't seem to smell a new scent, 'Wayo now. Wayo.' Foxy looks up at him hopefully and wags his tail. Does he notice Mr Henry is now trembling? I return to the boat, remove a billhook, stride to the overhanging roots and moss to begin hacking. Foxy watches me, wondering what I'm up to. Mr Henry puts the muzzle on him and repeats '*wayo.*'

There is nothing there and no other way out of the cavity. The hole itself is smaller than one of our buckets so I'm soon hacking at rock and stop.

'It's a ...' I can't bear to say the word '*stoat*'. 'It must have scaled the cliff and gone into the forest,' I say.

There, in the undergrowth and trees, our lovable birds will be softly sleeping, neatly curled under tree roots, tucked into mossy stumps, folded under fallen trunks. Their mossy, green feathers will disguise them as they sleep snugly in beds of fern fronds, crumpled, stiff and toast-golden. But their cosy, musky smell will betray them.

We know that. We have put them there.

Such easy prey.

'Like a pudding on a plate,' says Mr Henry.

How many birds have we delivered to this place? It is no longer a refuge. It is a death trap. How many are already dead? How many are still to die?

Waves continue to wash in with soft sighs, drops of drizzle collect on fronds and branches, a single red leaf slumps onto the beach. It seems the same as usual, but it's not. Everything is utterly changed.

Mr Henry screws up his eyes and looks across at the other, nearby cliff, which has a ragged edge of struggling ferns, wineberry and supplejacks scrambling down.

'Wayo, boy, wayo,' he says again to Foxy, but the dog is still confused by Mr Henry's order, though he leaves him and tries to please by half-heartedly scrabbling across the rocks. He hasn't been taught to trace the scent of an intruder and looks at me, puzzled by Mr Henry's strange behaviour. I stand, wordless, not knowing what to do.

Mr Henry turns and takes two steps towards the boat then stops and turns back to stare at the roots and moss I chopped at.

He doesn't speak. He looks at the bank, the cliff, the crowded vegetation. He motions to me and we walk the length of beach, staring at the sand and dry driftwood the colour of ashes, then turn and walk back to the spot where we saw the animal. There are no other tracks. Just these. They give no more information.

We are numb.

'Nothing more we can see. Nothing more we can do than last time,' says Mr Henry. 'And nothing worked then.' He slumps against the gunwales of *Pūtangi* and we stand there wordlessly.

'Nothing worked,' he repeats. 'What else can we do?'

There is neither sound nor sign of life. Dark,

rounded mounds of bush brood on all sides and the dense silence is crushing and oppressive. We are two frail humans in the immensity of the fiord.

After a slow, heavy time he looks at me and nods. I stow the billhook, we push *Pūtangi* into the water. We start the long, long row back to Pigeon Island.

It's a mostly silent trip. The drizzle turns to rain and flattens the water. Mr Henry mutters about the things we tried after Charlie's sighting in January.

'Nothing taken, nothing caught. What else could we do then? What else can we do now?'

I can't think of anything.

'We know stoats are too quick for a dog,' he says. 'And the rugged bush gives them the advantage.' He looks at Foxy, sitting very still in his favourite spot. 'I doubt he'd even be able to catch sight of one among the trees.'

That's true, of course.

'There's little hope of me shooting one,' he adds, as I continue, to row.

Silence.

'There is nothing else we can do,' he says after a while. 'Except repeat what we have already done.'

And there's nothing I can say.

'Aarrrrhhhh,' comes from Mr Henry again. It comes from deep inside him and is the sound of terrible, unspeakable pain.

The weka family come begging as we trudge up the path. Mr Henry ignores them. The fire is out. I light it and stow the gear. There is enough food: vegetables in the garden, tinned bully in the larder, bread baked yesterday. I prepare dinner.

These are practical things I can do.

Mr Henry just sits.

Not even Piopio can get his attention.

'Andy lad,' he says after a time and in a broken voice. 'There is no possibility it could have crossed Acheron Passage from the mainland. I reckon it's eighty chains at its most narrow and the water's treacherous. That means it must have come by another route, by island hopping, by swimming from one island to another, and from there to another, and another. How could stoats have been moving from island to island without our noticing?'

I can't answer him.

'Failed,' he said. 'I have failed those who sent me here, I have failed myself. Worst of all I have failed our lovable, trusting, beautiful birds.' He turns away from me. He probably doesn't want me to see his pain.

'I now regard myself as a full-time failure,' he says.

He makes that noise again.

CHAPTER FOURTEEN

Date: October, 1896

Bird tally: I can't bear to think of how many.

Injuries tally: My heart hurts.

This is what's been happening:

A southerly storm came through after we saw the stoat and we've been shut inside the homestead for three days now, with non-stop gusty wind and sleet outside.

Because we can't go outside we mend everything we can find to mend: darning the netting on my bedroom window which screens out sandflies, replacing the metal screw holding the wobbly knob on the lid of the flour barrel, tacking new hobnails on our boots to give us better grip in the bush. I even put on my oilskins and go down to the boathouse to mend the loose rowlock on *Pūtangi*.

Our rest period isn't pleasant, though. In the middle of doing something Mr Henry will sometimes stop whatever it is and gaze off into space. Or he will lay down a tool and wander absently over to the window and stand there, staring, without speaking. He ignores Foxy and Piopio and doesn't look at the kākā and weka outside. He has written up his field notes, a short letter to his boss, Mr Maitland, and a long one to his friend, Mr Melland. Mr Henry is a very truthful person and he will have admitted we've seen a stoat. The report and letters will be sent on the *Hinemoa* when it comes and collects me.

After what's happened I don't know how I feel about leaving. I want to stay and catch the stoat: I know there is virtually no chance of catching it. I want to stay in Dusky Sound with Mr Henry and Foxy: I want to go to Dunedin and see my family again.

Nothing is fun the way it used to be. I keep green manuka smouldering to keep away the sandflies and it's making our eyes red and sore, but that's not the problem. Our eyes would be sore and red anyway. I make queen pudding again, using penguin eggs, stale bread, tinned cream and rhubarb jam, which should have been a treat, but we don't enjoy it.

Foxy mopes about, getting under our feet. He whimpers when we tell him off.

I think about being outside and moving in the bush with springy, spongy moss underfoot and feeling the dampness of the mists and low clouds collecting on my cheeks. I'd like to be listening and looking for kiwi and kākāpō, finding a feather or seeing a footprint. I'd like to smell the bush and stick my nose into the close, musky scent of a kākāpō. I'd like to be listening to the wash-sh-sh-sh, wash-sh-sh-sh of the waves on the prow of *Pūtangi* when it's calm with a small breeze and we're sailing up Wet Jacket Arm.

I'd like to hear a lonely, black-back gull wailing for a companion or hear the whoosh of air and splash made by dolphins as they inspect our boat. But we stay inside till the storm blows through.

Mr Henry says the same thing over and over.

'They are the oldest New Zealanders, Andrew,' (he's stopped calling me Andy lad). 'But their days are numbered.'

The weather clears and we are trying to catch the stoat. We do all the things we did last time – traps inside boxes, strychnine-laced fish and bird bodies, tethered chicks with anxious parents. We build little runs, which a stoat can get into but a weka can't get out of, and place young weka in them as bait.

We see tracks near the baited carcases, but we don't catch anything.

We look for tracks the way we used to look for birds.

Mr Henry carries his gun at all times.

We don't catch a stoat.

We don't even see a stoat.

We sit in silence in the evenings and it's like being in church. We think about the comical, strutting little kākāpō with their watchful, knowing eyes, their stuffy, musty, cosy smell and their extraordinary booming. We think about the roa, with its efficient waterproof coat of feathers and equally efficient crochet-hook beak prizing food from the earth. We think of the kiwi, soft, shy, little and almost invisible as it fossicks in moss and beech leaves and among ferns, using its nostrils and ears to find food.

All of them are a little bumbly, a little simple, compared to the soaring songbirds with their colourful coats and beautiful voices. And that's what makes them so vulnerable. They fit into this country and weather perfectly, but are completely defenceless against the stealthy new invaders.

Mr Henry is right, these funny, cheerful, self-sufficient little birds are doomed.

It seems to me the birds are like Mr Henry himself. Alone, shy, stoic, living in rain, storms, drizzle and ever tormenting sandflies on punishing land, by a violent sea, in unrelenting bush. Unique.

Mr *Sad-and-lonely* Henry, whose Life's Work lies in tatters around him.

The *Hinemoa* is due tomorrow and I am packed and ready to leave.

CHAPTER FIFTEEN

Date: October, 1896
Bird tally: Not birding.
Injuries tally: None of course, I'm back in town.

This is what's been happening:

This must be the noisiest place in the world.

On the trip home I thought the motor of the *Hinemoa,* and the shouting and noise of her sailors was unpleasantly loud but it was nothing compared to the noise of Dunedin when I arrive. There are people everywhere and they talk all the time – I honestly think some of them might just chat for the sake of it, not really having anything important to say at all. I'm not used to thinking and talking at the same time and I find it hard with so much chatter all around.

What makes it worse are the ringing tram bells,

with people running to get on and shouting out to make it wait. Everywhere there seem to be dogs yapping, men calling, kids yelling, hawkers bawling. Sometimes a door will open and I hear music – it could be a gramophone, or a person singing. It's sale day and while animals bleat, moo and neigh there are men riding horses, leading horses, driving horses and carts. There is the puffing and whistle of the train to Port Chalmers. Everybody and everything seems to be rushing! No doubt there'll soon be one of those motor cars I've read about here and I bet they turn out to be just as noisy and rushy.

It was usually quiet in Dusky Sound – except for bird calls which were musical. And if it wasn't stormy it was often very still.

I miss the quietness and stillness.

Apart from all that noise in the middle of town it is good to be home with my family in Glen Road.

'You must make a point of writing to Mr Henry

every month,' says Mother. 'He will be so disappointed about the stoat, and probably lonely now you are gone.'

Father says he is proud of my achievements and pleased about my career decision.

Then I tell them what I've been wanting them to know. I tell them I can cook. 'Oh really,' Nancy says sniffily, and brings a cream-filled sponge to the table, placing it beside a lemon and coconut cake dripping with icing. 'What can you make?'

'I can catch and gut and cook fish, I can cook porridge, damper and scones. And rice.'

Nobody looks impressed.

'I can make scrambled penguin egg,' I add.

'That is absolutely disgusting,' says Nancy.

The twins make gagging noises till Mother hushes them.

Victoria wrinkles her nose. 'Can you make steak and kidney pie or apple strudel?' she asks, and then adds in a sickly-sweet voice 'Oh, do have some cake.'

Perhaps I should change the subject – luckily one of the twins does it for me. She asks if I've seen Arthur yet.

It is wonderful to be talking to Arthur again. When we first saw each other we both laughed because we look different from the way we looked before I left. Arthur is much taller and has a little moustache – and he says I am a different shape and walk in a different way. I suppose that's from all the work clambering around bush, rowing, and leaping onto landing places. Then we spoke – and we both laughed again, because we each have deeper voices now. It's a long, long time since I've had a friend to laugh with and it makes me joyful, so I laugh again for the pleasure of having a friend to laugh with. And that makes him laugh again.

I tell him about the birds and what a bird chase feels like. I tell him about sandflies and storms and rats – and about the time I woke up to find a rat sidling its nose into my ear. He asks lots of questions and says he wants me to teach him some of my skills, like how to sharpen a billhook or knife, sail a boat, train a dog to hunt with a muzzle. That leads me to telling him about Lassie.

'If I was lonely I'd talk to her and she would push up against me and make little whiny noises, but if she heard the word "bird" she'd sit straight up, thump her tail and look hard at me as if to say I'm ready, let's go. Let's go now!'

Arthur really is interested in everything I have to say so I tell him about the animal Charlie saw and thought was a weasel, but Mr Henry thought the one we saw was a stoat and the tracks confirmed it. I tell him how I feel we have failed, and how I am worried about Mr Henry's disappointment and loneliness.

'Andrew,' Arthur says to me. 'I have liked listening to you but now I want to say something.'

I'm surprised as this is not the way we used to talk to each other, but I nod.

'Mr Henry and you might think you've failed, but

you don't know that you have. The birds are still there in Fiordland: correct?'

I nod.

'And even though there may be stoats and or weasels in Fiordland, the birds might be all right in other places, on islands, high in the mountains, in isolated areas: correct?'

Another nod.

'And you and Mr Henry know all about them, what they eat, how they breed, how to capture them, how to keep them in captivity: correct?'

'Yes.'

'And all that information, as well as his field notes, his newspaper articles, his photos, sketches, maps and records have been sent to the Acclimatisation Society and properly filed, so it won't be lost but will always be available for future reference?'

'Yes.'

'In years to come, Andrew, maybe when people think they are extinct, some more kākāpō will be found, maybe near Milford Sound or maybe on Stewart Island. When that happens, because no one has seen a kākāpō for so long, the work you both did and Mr Henry's information about them will be invaluable. They will need his material about capturing and rescuing those birds, assisting them to breed, keeping them safe. His notes will ensure they do not become extinct.'

I like what he's saying. Maybe all our work won't have been wasted. I feel better already.

'You might be right,' I say. 'One day they might use information from our work to save the kākāpō. And they might be so grateful they name the first one they rescue "Richard Henry".'

'Maybe they will,' said Arthur. 'Maybe they will,' he repeats. 'And maybe someone will write a book about Andrew Burt and title it *Kākāpō Keeper*.'

THE TRUE STORY

You have read a story based on fact.

Richard Henry existed.

He lived in Dusky Sound (then often called Dusky Bay, which is what Captain Cook named it) from 1894 till 1908 and tried to save the kākāpō, tokoeka and kiwi pukupuku from what appeared to be immediate extinction.

He employed four different boys as assistants. (I have compressed the time frame and combined all the boys into one character to simplify the story. The name of Andrew's 'friend', Arthur Deans, is actually the name of Richard Henry's last helper.)

Despite his work and dedication mustelids did invade Resolution and the other islands of Dusky Sound.

However, though he may have died thinking he had failed to save endangered, ground-dwelling birds, the knowledge gained from his work was crucial almost 100 years later when conservationists successfully saved the kākāpō species from extinction.

Richard Henry was born in 1845 in Ireland and while still a child travelled with his family to Australia, where he developed a love of wildlife. He came to New Zealand during the 1870s and continued to observe and study native birds while working in various parts of the country. In 1883 he moved to Te Anau and found work as a carpenter, rabbiter, boatman and guide as well as continuing his interest in wildlife. While he was there he developed a close friendship with Edward Melland and his family, of Te Anau Downs Station, and wrote articles about local fauna for the *Otago Witness*.

He was appointed caretaker and curator (and soon after was also warranted as a ranger in case of seal poaching) of Dusky Sound in 1894.

Title: On the watch (c1900)

Richard Henry standing in front of his boatshed and alongside Pūtangi in Boatshed Bay, Pigeon Island.[2]

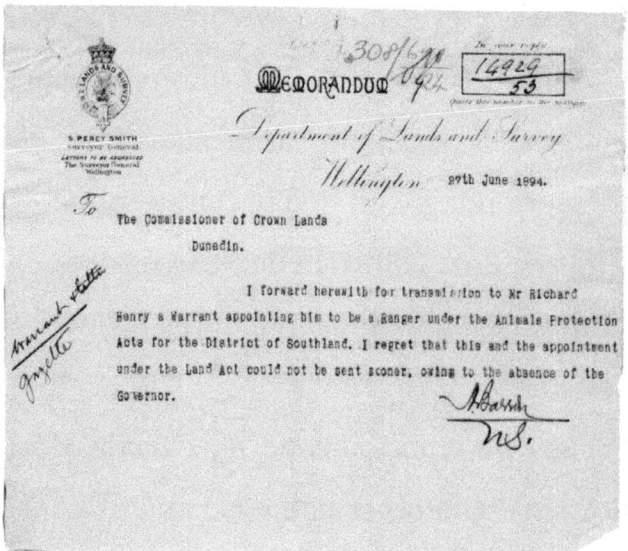

The warrant of appointment as a Crown Lands Ranger.[3]

At that time newly arrived mustelids were decimating native birds and his task was to catch the most vulnerable species, the ground-dwelling kākāpō and kiwi, and relocate them to Resolution Island. Resolution Island was chosen because people believed no predator would be able to swim across Acheron Passage (a really rough, dangerous channel, 560 metres wide at its narrowest point) which separates the island from the mainland. Other animals had escaped into the bush – rats, cats and dogs – and they also preyed on the defenceless native birds.

Richard Henry had four different apprentices, or 'boys' or 'assistants', as he sometimes described them, working with him in Dusky Sound. The first, Andrew Burt (18) travelled to Dusky Sound with him, stayed for eighteen months and was of great assistance.

The two who followed him, Davie Mowat and Gordon — (no other name is known), each stayed for less than six months and were not suited to

(Copy)

ESTIMATE OF OUTFIT FOR RESOLUTION ISLAND.

```
One half-decked Sailing Boat (but not required at present) . .£25  0  0
One 16 feet Dingey . . . . . . . . . . . . . . . . . . . . . . 10  0  0
One 12 by 10 Tent and Fly, and one 8 by 10 ditto . . . . . . .  4  0  0
Bushman's Tools,- axes, crosscut saw, pick, shovel, spade, bill-
       hooks, maul, wedges and shingle knife . . . . . . . .    4  0  0
200 yards Wire Netting . . . . . . . . . . . . . . . . . . . . 4  0  0
Roofing Iron . . . . . . . . . . . . . . . . . . . . . . . . . 3  0  0
       If a house is to be built and a piece of garden cleared,
    it might be well to employ an assistant for 3 months at a
    cost of say . . . . . . . . . . . . . . . . . . . . . . . 20  0  0
       But I am perfectly able and willing to do it myself if
    I have time.                                               70  0  0
```

I would also suggest that provisions be supplied from Government stores as to Light-house Keepers, because it would be much cheaper; and then you can decide on the salary you think sufficient.

There are many other things I would like to have, such as a code of signals, telescope, barometer, thermometer, rain-guage, chart and compass &c. but I suppose I should pay for these.

If you think this too much you might strike out the larger boat, but then I would be confined to the two sounds, and it would ultimately be needed, so I thought it well to go in the bill at first.

Then there is freight and passage to be added. I could not get the price from the Union Coy. nor Keith Ramsay, but may do so to-day. Possibly the U.S.S. Coy. might let one of their steamers land me on their way to Milford.

The wire netting is to form enclosures to hold live birds caught on the main-land for removal to out-lying islands or to go away in the Hinemoa.

The roofing iron would be very useful at a new camp and is easily removed to roof the house.

I would propose a house of two rooms and a store, with iron fire-place. Material for house to cost about £15 to £20.

I would leave a list of Timber &c. to go down when the site is fixed.

                                        Yours respectfully,

                                        (Signed)   R. HENRY.

Messrs Maitland and Chapman.   3rd Feb. 1894.
     Dunedin.

List of materials required to build the house on Pigeon Island.[4]

the work. The visit of the *Cavalier* with the young passenger, Charlie Johnston, who claimed to have seen a weasel, took place in March 1900, and assistant Gordon left on her return voyage. (We do not know anything at all about the real Charlie, this is a fictional interpretation. In fact all of the characters in *Kākāpō Keeper* are imagined interpretations of real people.) Richard Henry was actually on his own in August, 1900 when he himself saw a stoat on Resolution Island.

Arthur Deans came for three months in January, 1901 and was highly regarded by Richard Henry. After Arthur's departure the disappointed old man lived on alone, still employed as caretaker of Resolution Island.

He continued to act as conservator of all native birds but no longer attempted to move them to sanctuary – it seemed there wasn't one. As a government employee he was obliged to provide bird skins and feathers, and live birds, for collectors, museums and

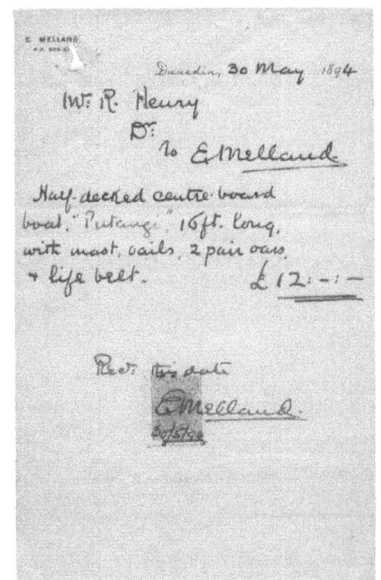

Receipt of purchase for the Pūtangi for £12.00 (around $25.00), which would equate to around $2,500.00 today.[5]

TRANSCRIPT OF THE EXTRACT FROM RICHARD HENRY'S NOTES SEEN BELOW:

There is a mad north wind sometimes and I have taken the mast out of my boat and intend to go without it. The wind comes in puffs of fearful force which lasts for a few seconds at a time. I have braced and strengthened our hut until it looks like a stockade but there has been no wind lately, though we had it once a week at first. [6]

aviaries when instructed to do so. (At the time, that sort of activity was regarded as 'scientific investigation' and accepted as being a necessary way of gathering information.)

He spent a lot of this time writing: about New Zealand birds, his boyhood memories of Australian wildlife, the current political situation, essays, and commentaries on a variety of subjects. He assembled his ornithological notes into an illustrated manuscript for an authoritative book titled *The Habits of the Flightless Birds of New Zealand;* much of it was published by the Lands and Survey Department and parts of it were published in Australia and America.

As a ranger he was expected to prevent any illegal killing of native birds or seals. This was a frustrating task for one man on his own. Groups regarded it as a 'sport' to go there on shooting excursions and although there was a ban on sealing, 'poachers' were known to try to capture them and sell their skins. Things became even more difficult when commercial

A requisition signed by Richard Henry.[7]

fishermen with freezers on their boats began arriving – it was impossible to know exactly what they were doing. Some of them, and a few tourists, regarded it as a joke to tell him they had released dogs on Resolution Island and he could never take such a threat lightly. Prospectors looking for minerals often took dogs into the area and when the government attempted to build a track from Supper Cove to Lake Manapouri, some of the roadmen hunted birdlife with dogs they owned.

In 1905, over two million acres in south-west of the South Island ('Fiordland') were reserved for a proposed national park, though this did not formally happen until 1952.

Over the years various laws were passed to protect native wildlife.

In 2008 the Department of Conservation began an intense vermin-eradication programme on Resolution Island.

Although Richard Henry stayed on after he had seen the stoat, his spirit took a severe beating, for

Above: Title: Kitchen (c.1900) - interior of Richard Henry's home on Pigeon Island .[8]

Below: the small peninsula on Pigeon Island, on which he built his house, also showing the boatshed near the water in lower front right, and the storehouse between the two buildings.[9]

he believed the birds he loved and had hoped to save were doomed. Eventually, in 1908, he left and took on the role of caretaker on Kapiti Island, where he stayed for three years until moving to Katikati, then to Helensville where he lived until his death in 1929.

But Richard Henry's work was not all in vain.

For many years kākāpō teetered on the edge of extinction. There was an unsuccessful 1960s attempt to maintain a captive population but by the 1970s none were known to exist in the wild. This changed when eighteen were discovered in the Milford Sound area; disappointingly, these all turned out to be male. Then more were discovered on Stewart Island and a recovery team used the information Henry had so carefully and painstakingly composed to successfully capture and keep them. Their recovery has been slow and steady and there are now surviving birds on Whenua Hou (Codfish), Maud and Little Barrier islands. All birds are individually named and monitored.

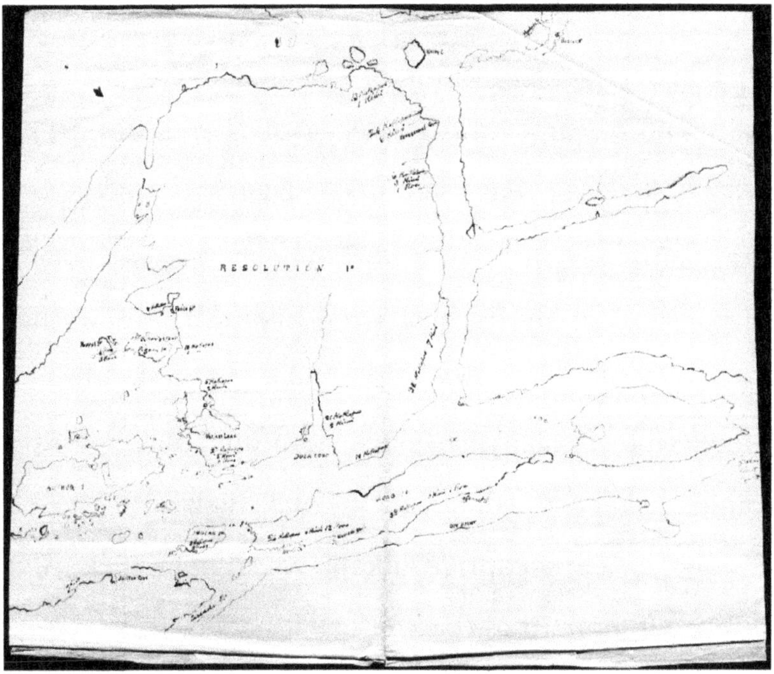

Above: Richard Henry's hand-drawn sketch of the area covered by his research and rescue. [10]

Below: Mr R. Henry's residence, Pigeon Island (c.1900) taken from Sandy Bay, on the other side of the Peninsula with his tame weka in the foreground. [11]

Modern conservationists acknowledge the work done by Richard Henry, who made extraordinarily exact observations of not just the kākāpō but other rare birds like the piopio (now extinct), takahē, South Island kōkako, and the bush wren. Interestingly, though some of his field notes were disputed at the time, modern technology has since vindicated his theories about kākāpō breeding, nesting and chick raising.

The very first captive kākāpō was named Richard Henry in honour of the work that he did.

Readers may have met Sirocco (see page 228), an ambassador for the kākāpō species, who prefers humankind to that of his cousins and has travelled to many parts of New Zealand and met many young New Zealanders.

If you would like to know more about the work on Whenua Hou/Codfish Island, the kākāpō recovery programme and how you can help, check the internet – www.kakaporecovery.org.nz is a good place to start – or you can read *Kākāpō: Rescued from the brink of extinction* by Alison Ballance. Alison Ballance has also produced a wonderful podcast called *Kākāpō Files*.

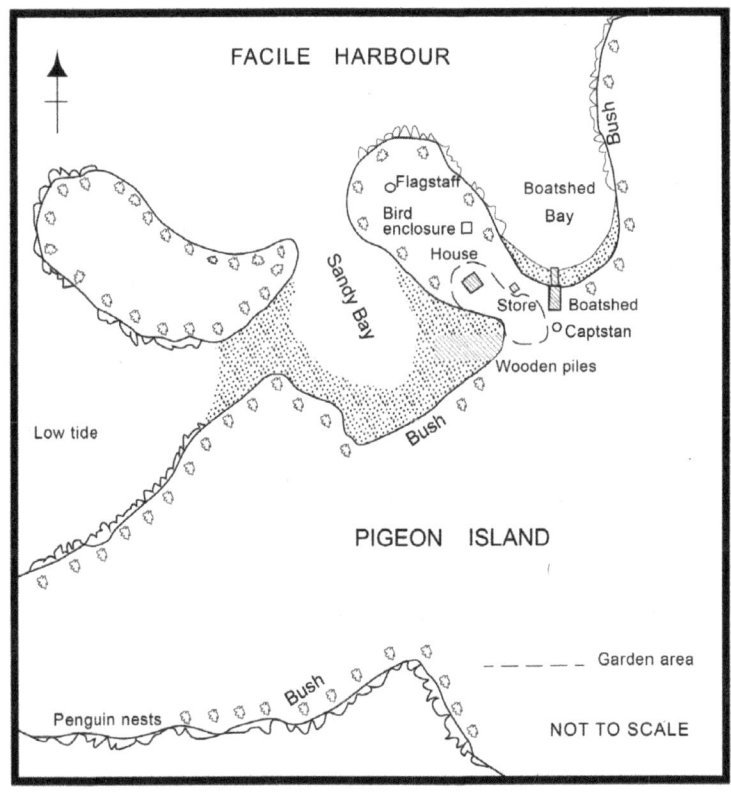

Map of Henry's house, services and outbuildings on Pigeon Island.[12]

The order opposite[13] is for 'roa' and was made because it was thought they might rid paddocks and vegetable plots of wireworms. That was a practical use, but people also wanted birds to stuff and display as decoration (in which case the more beautiful, the better) or to be part of 'scientific' collections (in which case the more rare, the better).

Because of this fashion, during the 1800s, naturalists from all around the world wanted skins of New Zealand birds to stuff and display in homes, private collections, and museums. In 1900, for example, Uchter Knox, Earl of Ranfurly and Governor of New Zealand, asked Richard Henry to collect specimens of the following birds for the British Museum:

fantails	wrens	sparrow hawks
tomtits	roa	black woodhen
yellowheads	kākāpō	brown creepers
robins	parakeet	red-fronted parakeet
warblers	native thrush	orange-wattled crows

Department of Agriculture,

Wellington, N.Z., June 17th, 1897.

Sir,-

My attention has been drawn to a statement made by Mr Henry regarding the habits of the "Roa". He suggests that it might be useful in gardens and orchards in destroying insects. I shall be glad if you will communicate with Mr Henry and ask him if possible to secure a few pairs.

I have the honour to be,

Sir,

Your obedient Servant,

John D Ritchie

Secretary.

The Secretary,

Otago Acclimatisation Society,

D U N E D I N.

NOTE FOR READERS

Most of the information on which this book is based can be found in the Dunedin Regional Office of Archives New Zealand, which holds a lot of papers and reports written by, and pertaining to, Richard Henry's employment in Dusky Sound and is available at the online database of Archives NZ:

www.archway.archives.govt.nz

I loved reading an amazing book called *Richard Henry of Resolution Island,* a biography written by Susanne and John Hill and published by John McIndoe, Dunedin, in association with the New Zealand Wildlife Service, in 1987.

Please note also that in Richard Henry's time
- many English-speaking people made Māori nouns plural by adding 's'. I have not done that.
- many Māori words were written without the macron above a long vowel as in kākāpō. I have not done that.
- what we would call *tokoeka* (southern brown kiwi) Richard Henry called roa. I have kept his name.
- people used imperial measurements and I have kept them to fit the times.

    one inch = 2.5 centimetres

    one foot (ft) = 30.48 centimetres

    one yard = 1 metre (just under)

    one chain = 20 metres (just over)

    one mile = 1.6 kilometres

EQUIPMENT

Billhook –

A billhook is a traditional cutting tool used for cutting small, woody material like shrubs and branches. It has a shorter handle than the more commonly known 'slasher' which has a heavy blade and is used for 'slashing' down scrub, undergrowth, etc.

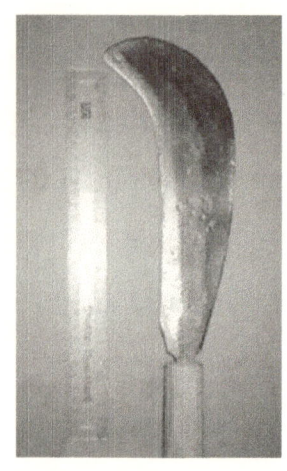

Billhook of the type used by Richard Henry and his apprentices [14]

Camp Oven –

A thick-walled cooking pot with a tight-fitting lid, which allows for adding hot coals from the fire to be piled on top. Camp ovens are usually made of seasoned cast iron.

Camp oven [15]

THE BIRDS

Kākā –

These very noisy, olive-brown parrots display a vivid, reddish orange under the wing and crimson under the body, with a grey-white crown. Their call is usually loud and grating but can be melodious, or just a straight note. They nest, feed and live in forest trees and often move in flocks. They eat insects (especially wood-boring ones like huhu), and the seeds, flowers and fruits of some native beech and podocarp.

Photo: James Mortimer

Kākāpō (or 'ground parrot' in nineteenth-century New Zealand) –

At about 60cm tall this is the largest, most distinctive, and probably the rarest, parrot. Its plumage is mottled, with a dark-green head and upper parts, lighter back and wings, and light greenish-yellow underparts. Kākāpō wings are lemon-yellow, streaked darker and its legs are yellowish. It has a facial disc like an owl and whiskers like a cat. It does not fly, but is an agile climber, and lives on mountains, high areas and river flats up to scrub at 1,000 metres. It is nocturnal, solitary, and breeds irregularly (when the podocarp forests seed, known as a 'mast' year).

Unlike most parrots it is not monogamous and males gather at night on a system of tracks and bowls for a 'lek' display – to dance and 'boom' their presence. This is done by inflation of the thorax, which is marked by a series of grunts, then loud booming when the thorax has reached its maximum inflation. Booming commences late November or early

Sirocco (an adult male kākāpō) - Maud Island

Photo: Dylan Winkel, NZ Birds Online

December and continues till approximately mid-February. Their drumming sound attracts females who will make their choice, nest under tree stumps or logs, then raise their young as a single parent during the winter when the fruit ripens.

Mothers are fiercely protective of their young but males play no part in the chicks' upbringing.

Rimu drupes are a staple food but kākāpō also eat a wide range of vegetation such as tutu and fuchsia berries. It grazes like a rabbit.

Kiwi –

When Richard Henry lived on Pigeon Island he divided the two sorts of kiwi he rescued into 'grey kiwi', (kiwi pukupuku, which we also call the little spotted kiwi) and 'roa' (which we know as tokoeka, the South Island brown kiwi).

Photo: Keith Beck

Tokoeka – A soft, shaggy bird, which has black-streaked, grey-brown plumage, whiskers, and a very long, pale beak with nostrils on the end. Mostly nocturnal and living on tussock grassland, in scrub or native forest, it has short legs, no tail and doesn't fly. Tokoeka eat worms and invertebrates and sometimes fallen fruit

Piopio (also called native thrush) –

An extinct, olive-brown bird which had white streaks below, a rusty-coloured rump and long, dark-brown legs. It lived in native forests and was about twice the size of the introduced thrush. Piopio has been described as having the most beautiful call of any New Zealand bird, and as being very good at imitating other birds. It was said to be unafraid of humans and omnivorous, eating worms, insects, spiders, fruit seeds, mosses and grass. Captive birds even ate potato and meat.

Photo: Te Papa Exhibition / Department of Conservation / NZ Birds Online

Pūtangitangi (also called paradise ducks) –
These belong to the group known as shelducks which have the characteristics of both ducks and geese. They are easy to recognise because of the female's white head, though the male shows beautiful, more subtle tones of chestnut, brown and black. They were uncommon in the nineteenth century but as they are grazing birds, modern farming practices have helped them. They also eat pond plants and aquatic insects and are about 60 cm high.

Photo: Oscar Thomas

Tawaki (Fiordland crested penguin) –

Usually about 60cm tall, it is blueish-black on its upper body with white underneath and pink feet. The head is black with a boad yellow eyebrow stripe which starts at the nostril and goes past its eyes to droop down its neck. It's found in coastal forest, scrub and caves of South Westland, Fiordland, Stewart Island and nearby islands, where it feeds on krill, octopus, squid and small fish.

Photo: DOC - Anthony Behren

Photo: Glenda Rees

THE MAMMALS

Rats –

All rats have fur, short legs and pointed noses. Three types of rat live in New Zealand.

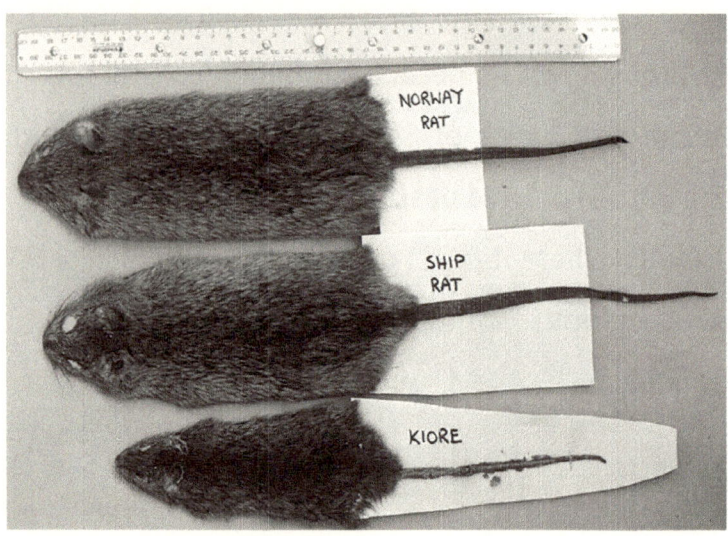

Exhibit: Peter E. Smith

The Norway rat (also known as the brown rat, common rat, wharf rat, or sewer rat) –

This the largest rat found in New Zealand. Its tail is about 180mm long and can be as long as its body, which is usually about 200mm in length. It weighs up to one kilo. It has coarse fur, usually brown or dark-grey, and the underparts are a lighter colour.

It is active at night and a good swimmer but poor climber. It is an omnivore with cereals forming a substantial part of its diet. It probably came from China, not Norway, inhabits sewers and burrows, and lives in hierarchical groups.

<u>Ship rat</u> (sometimes called the black rat) –

A rodent that has a tail longer than its body and has larger ears, large enough to be folded over its eyes. It is usually black to light brown with lighter undersides. It is a poor swimmer but a great climber, often nesting in trees and having litters of six to twelve young. The ship rat, being a good tree climber, nocturnal and inconspicuous, is deadly to birds.

Both these species are associated with human activity and are found in houses, tips, waterways, and cropland. Ship rats are cleaner, not inhabiting rubbish dumps like Norwegian rats.

<u>Polynesian rat</u> (kiore) –

One that has a tail proportionately longer than a ship rat and looks like a cross between a ship rat and a mouse. It is found in many parts of the Pacific including Fiordland, Stewart Island and some offshore islands. It was introduced to New Zealand by Māori settlers. Kiore is recognised as a predator of native insects, lizards and birds, a browser of native flora and an agricultural pest.

All rats have dealt, and continue to deal, immeasurable harm to native insect and bird life.

Exhibit: DOC – D Garrick

Weasels, Stoats and Ferrets –

During the second half of the nineteenth century, the South Island of New Zealand was overrun with rabbits.

Dogs and traps failed to get rid of them so landowners wanted their natural enemies – ferrets, stoats and weasels – introduced from Europe, and from 1882 the government began importing mustelids.

Mustelids are slim, agile, alert and highly efficient predators. They range in size:

<u>Weasels:</u> are the smallest, about 20-25 centimetres long (sleek, brown with light underparts). They don't like bush and haven't thrived as well in New Zealand.

<u>Stoats:</u> are about 35–40 centimetres long (brown and white, sometimes turning white in winter, with a black-tip on the tail). They are about half the size of a rabbit and live anywhere.

<u>Ferrets:</u> the largest, are about 50 centimetres long (with dark facial mask and a shaggy coat of creamy yellow, often a black tipped tail). They are the size of a small cat and live in pastoral areas, scrub and forest edges.

These animals found native birds to be an easy prey and in no time the native, ground-dwelling birds began to disappear. In 1891 lobby groups – especially the Otago Acclimatisation Society – began arguing for an island haven to save native birds from the new predators.

Because ferrets were known to have a strong sense of smell and to be good swimmers, they insisted the island chosen could not be too close to the shores of the mainland.

New Zealand's seventh-largest island, Resolution, in Dusky Sound, was regarded as a suitable refuge, especially as the rare, ground-dwelling birds of the south-west fiords – kākāpō, two species of kiwi, weka and takahē (though it was thought the last might already be extinct) – lived nearby.

In August 1892 the government agreed to make Resolution Island a reserve and to employ a custodian.

Richard Henry was appointed to the position. He took up residence on Pigeon Island, near Resolution Island, in July of 1894.

ENDNOTES

1 *Lassie ready for work* in Henry, Richard: *Photographs of Dusky Sound*. Reference No: P1966-004-005. Hocken Collections, Uare Taoka o Hākena, University of Otago – image page 51.

2 *On the watch* in Henry, Richard : *Photographs of Dusky Sound* in P1966-004. Reference No: P1966-004-001a. Hocken Collections, Uare Taoka o Hākena, University of Otago – image page 207.

3 *DAAK D202/1a 0401 (R1269771)* - Archives New Zealand Te Rua Mahara o te Kāwanatanga, Dunedin Regional Office – image page 207.

4 *DAAK D202/1a 0427 (R1269771)* - Archives New Zealand Te Rua Mahara o te Kāwanatanga, Dunedin – image page 209.

5 *DAAK D202/1a 0399 (R1269771)* – Archives New Zealand Te Rua Mahara o te Kāwanatanga, Dunedin – image page 211

6 *DAAK D202/1a 0368 (R1269771)* – Archives New Zealand Te Rua Mahara o te Kāwanatanga, Dunedin – image 211

7 *DAAK D202/1a 0382 (R1269771)* – Archives New Zealand Te Rua Mahara o te Kāwanatanga, Dunedin – image page 213.

8 *Kitchen (c 1900)* in Henry, Richard: *Photographs of Dusky Sound* Reference No: P1966-004-004. Hocken Collections, Uare Taoka o Hākena, University of Otago – image page 215

9 *Mr R. Henry's residence, Pigeon Island* in Henry, Richard : *Photographs of Dusky Sound*. Reference No: P1966-004-002. Hocken Collections, Uare Taoka o Hākena, University of Otago – image page 215.

10 *DAAK D202/1a 0322 (R1269771)* – Archives New Zealand Te Rua Mahara o te Kāwanatanga, Dunedin – image page 217.

11 *Mr R. Henry's residence, Pigeon Island* in Henry, Richard : *Photographs of Dusky Sound*. Reference No: P1966-004-002. Hocken Collections, Uare Taoka o Hākena, University of Otago – image page 217.

12 *Diagram based on the drawing in 'Richard Henry of Resolution Island' by Susanne and John Hill. Published by John McIndoe* – image page 234.

13 *DAAK D202/1a 0226 (R1269771)* – Archives New Zealand Te Rua Mahara o te Kāwanatanga, Dunedin Regional Office – image page 221.

14 *Billhook https://en.wiktionary.org/wiki/billhook* – image page 224.

15 *Camp fire with dutch oven – creative commons* – image page 224.

ACKNOWLEDGMENTS

I would like to acknowledge both the New Zealand Society of Authors Te Puni Kaituhi O Aotearoa (PEN NZ Inc) and Creative New Zealand for the receipt of a mentoring award.

Philippa Werry was my mentor and I appreciated her unfailingly sage advice, which she couched in such positive terms.

I also the appreciate time and encouragement I received from Nanette Monin, Jim Dawson, Owen Buckingham and members of my writing group – Ann, Anne, Chris, Donna, Jane, Kymberley and Laura.

I want to acknowledge sturdy *Time Bandit* and her skipper, and time spent sailing in brooding, numinous Dusky Sound.

Thank you, too, Keith Beck and the other photographers and writers who have been generous with material and advice, as well as the general helpfulness of staff at the Dunedin branch of Archives New Zealand, Te Rua Mahara o te Kāwanatanga and the Hocken Library, Uare Taoka o Hākena, University of Otago.

ABOUT THE AUTHOR

GAY BUCKINGHAM

Born in the south of the South Island, Gay's short stories have been broadcast by Radio New Zealand and published in the *Dominion Post*, *Turbine*, *takahē* Magazine and *Sunday Star Times*, as well as online and in anthologies. She is author of *The Grand Electrification of the South*, commissioned and published by The Power Company Limited, Invercargill, and has also written non-fiction for *Memories* magazine. Her children's stories have been broadcast by Radio New Zealand and she has had minor successes in competitions in various genres including poetry, short, and very short, stories – some of her writing has even been set to music!

Gay is a graduate of the University of Otago, has an MA in Creative Writing from the IIML, Victoria University of Wellington and is (mostly) domiciled in Dunedin. She enjoys the natural world and has spent time on a yacht in Dusky Sound.